D1373385

# TO THE DEATH!

Writer: STAN LEE
Penciler: JACK KIRBY

Inkers: VINCE COLLETTA & BILL EVERETT
Colorist: MATT MILLA
Letterers: ART SIMEK & SAM ROSEN

Cover Artists: OLIVIER COIPEL, MARK MORALES
& LAURA MARTIN

Collection Editors: MARK D. BEAZLEY & CORY LEVINE
Assistant Editors: ALEX STARBUCK & NELSON RIBEIRO
Editor, Special Projects: JENNIFER GRÜNWALD
Senior Editor, Special Projects: JEFF YOUNGQUIST
SVP of Print & Digital Publishing Sales: DAVID GABRIEL
Research: JEPH YORK & DANA PERKINS
Select Art Reconstruction: TOM ZIUKO
Production: JERRON QUALITY COLOR & JOE FRONTIRRE
Book Designer: SPRING HOTELING

Editor In Chief: AXEL ALONSO
Chief Creative Officer: JOE QUESADA
Publisher: DAN BUCKLEY
Executive Producer: ALAN FINE

SPECIAL THANKS TO RALPH MACCHIO

**Visit us at www.abdopublishing.com**

Reinforced library bound editions published in 2014 by Spotlight, a division of the ABDO Group, PO Box 398166, Minneapolis, MN 55439.  Spotlight produces high-quality reinforced library bound editions for schools and libraries. Published by agreement with Marvel Characters, Inc.

Printed in the United States of America, North Mankato, Minnesota.
042013
092013
♻ This book contains at least 10% recycled material.

marvel.com
© 2013 Marvel

**Library of Congress Cataloging-in-Publication Data**

Lee, Stan.
 To the death! / story by Stan Lee ; art by Jack Kirby.
    pages cm. -- (Thor, tales of Asgard)
 "Marvel."
 Summary: An adaptation, in graphic novel form, of comic books revealing the adventures of the Norse Gods and Thor before he came to Earth, featuring a battle between the godling and his friends and the evil ruler, Mogul.
 ISBN 978-1-61479-173-7 (alk. paper)
 1.  Thor (Norse deity)--Juvenile fiction. 2.  Graphic novels. [1. Graphic novels. 2. Thor (Norse deity)--Fiction. 3. Mythology, Norse--Fiction.] I. Kirby, Jack, illustrator. II. Title.
 PZ7.S81712To 2013
 741.5'973--dc23
                        2013005407

All Spotlight books are reinforced library bindings
and manufactured in the United States of America.

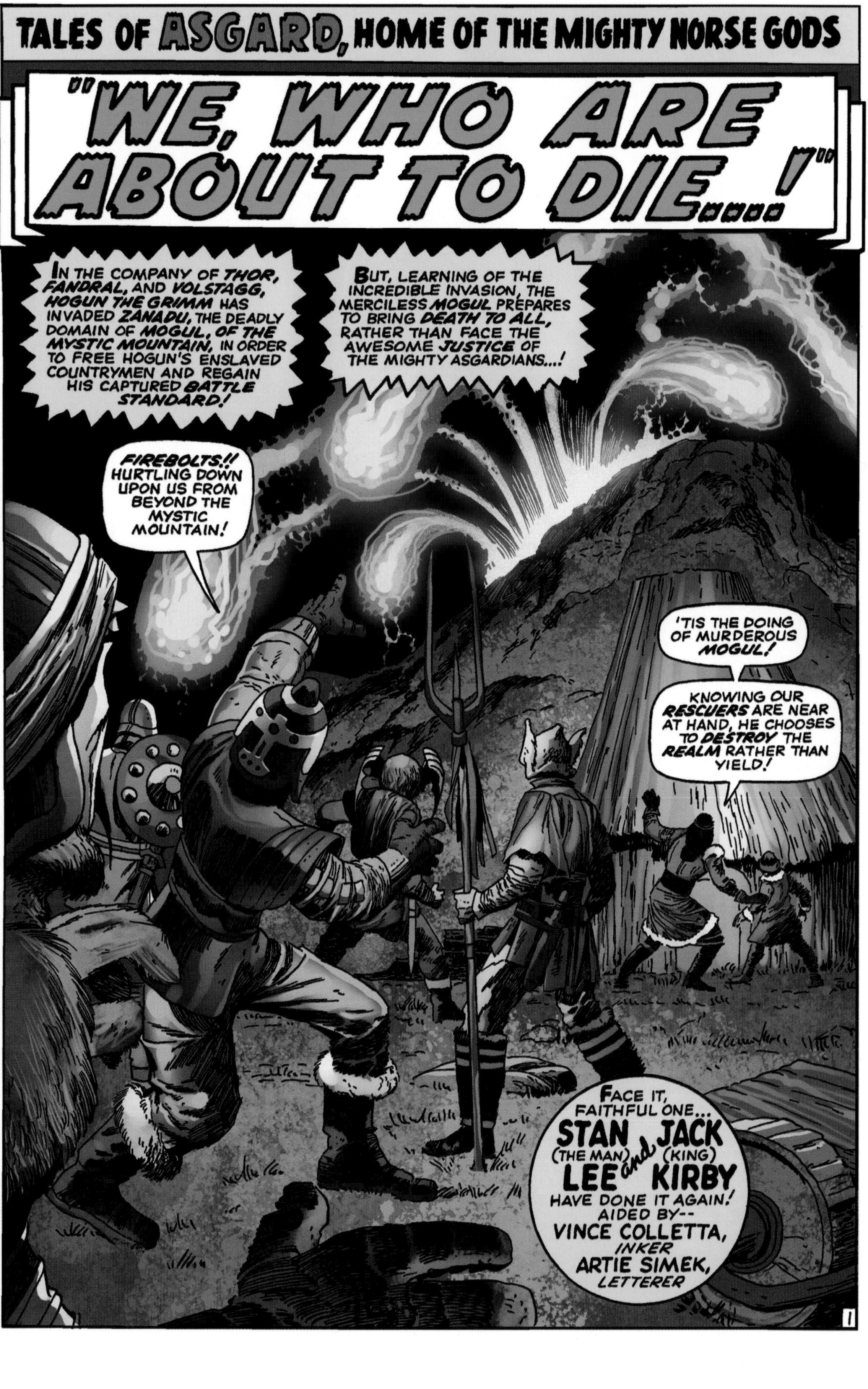

TALES OF ASGARD, HOME OF THE MIGHTY NORSE GODS
"WE, WHO ARE ABOUT TO DIE...!"
IN THE COMPANY OF THOR, FANDRAL, AND VOLSTAGG, HOGUN THE GRIMM HAS INVADED ZANADU, THE DEADLY DOMAIN OF MOGUL, OF THE MYSTIC MOUNTAIN, IN ORDER TO FREE HOGUN'S ENSLAVED COUNTRYMEN AND REGAIN HIS CAPTURED BATTLE STANDARD!
BUT, LEARNING OF THE INCREDIBLE INVASION, THE MERCILESS MOGUL PREPARES TO BRING DEATH TO ALL, RATHER THAN FACE THE AWESOME JUSTICE OF THE MIGHTY ASGARDIANS...!
FIREBOLTS!! HURTLING DOWN UPON US FROM BEYOND THE MYSTIC MOUNTAIN!
'TIS THE DOING OF MURDEROUS MOGUL!
KNOWING OUR RESCUERS ARE NEAR AT HAND, HE CHOOSES TO DESTROY THE REALM RATHER THAN YIELD!
FACE IT, FAITHFUL ONE... STAN (THE MAN) LEE and JACK (KING) KIRBY HAVE DONE IT AGAIN! AIDED BY-- VINCE COLLETTA, INKER ARTIE SIMEK, LETTERER
1

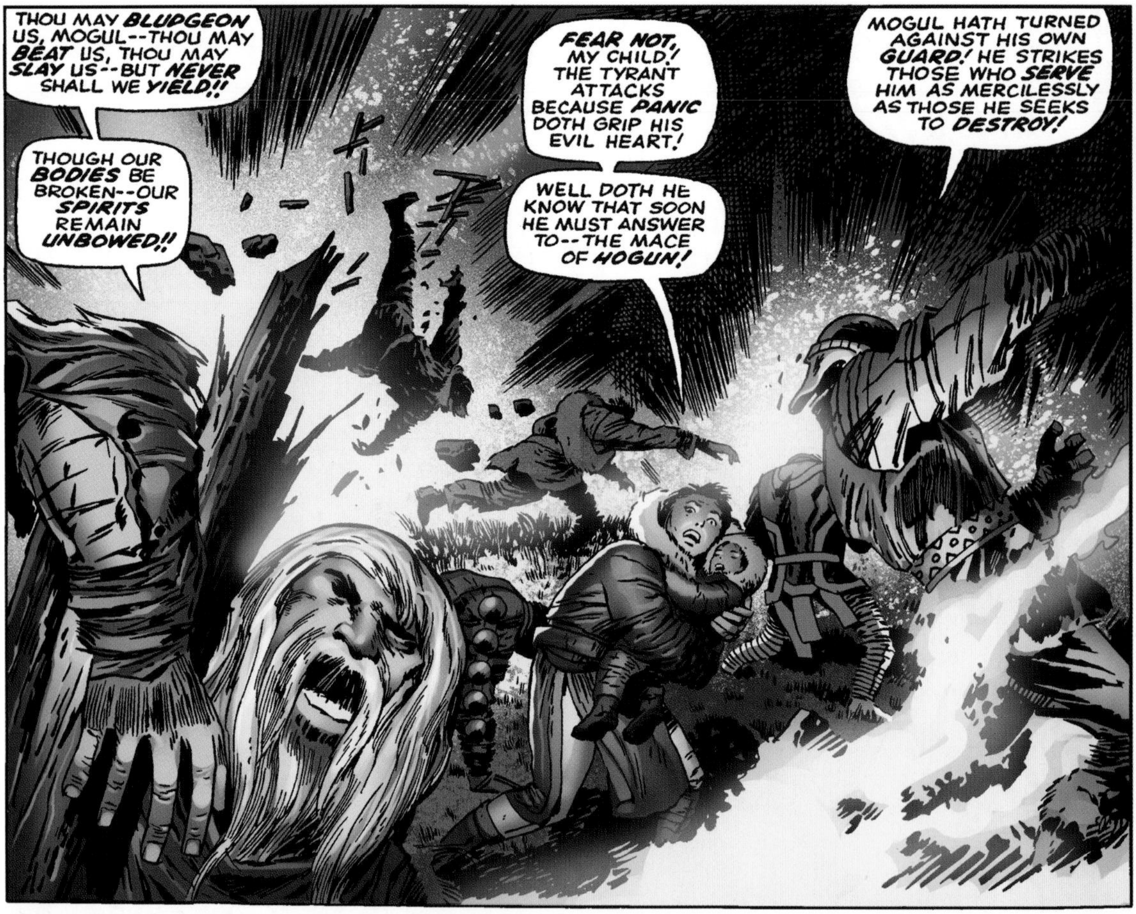
THOU MAY BLUDGEON US, MOGUL--THOU MAY BEAT US, THOU MAY SLAY US--BUT NEVER SHALL WE YIELD!!
THOUGH OUR BODIES BE BROKEN--OUR SPIRITS REMAIN UNBOWED!!
FEAR NOT, MY CHILD! THE TYRANT ATTACKS BECAUSE PANIC DOTH GRIP HIS EVIL HEART!
WELL DOTH HE KNOW THAT SOON HE MUST ANSWER TO--THE MACE OF HOGUN!
MOGUL HATH TURNED AGAINST HIS OWN GUARD! HE STRIKES THOSE WHO SERVE HIM AS MERCILESSLY AS THOSE HE SEEKS TO DESTROY!

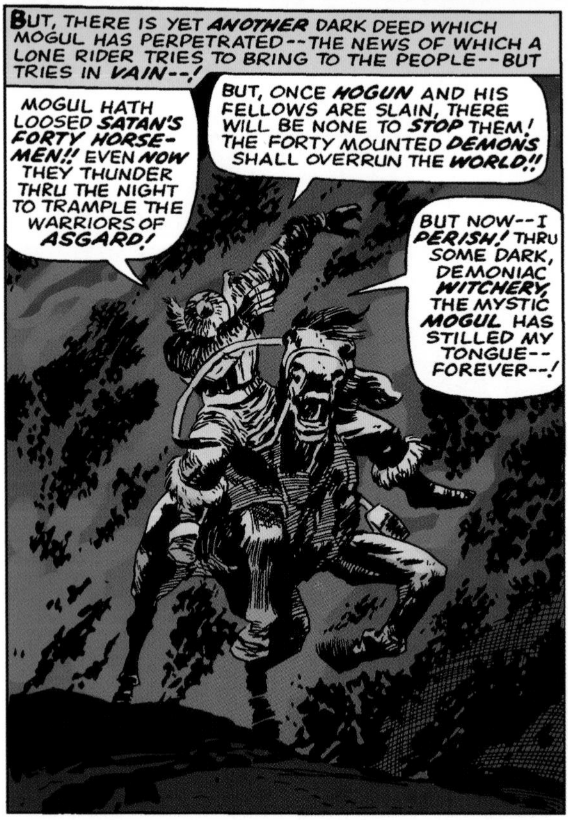
BUT, THERE IS YET ANOTHER DARK DEED WHICH MOGUL HAS PERPETRATED--THE NEWS OF WHICH A LONE RIDER TRIES TO BRING TO THE PEOPLE--BUT TRIES IN VAIN--!
MOGUL HATH LOOSED SATAN'S FORTY HORSE-MEN!! EVEN NOW THEY THUNDER THRU THE NIGHT TO TRAMPLE THE WARRIORS OF ASGARD!
BUT, ONCE HOGUN AND HIS FELLOWS ARE SLAIN, THERE WILL BE NONE TO STOP THEM! THE FORTY MOUNTED DEMONS SHALL OVERRUN THE WORLD!!
BUT NOW--I PERISH! THRU SOME DARK, DEMONIAC WITCHERY, THE MYSTIC MOGUL HAS STILLED MY TONGUE--FOREVER--!

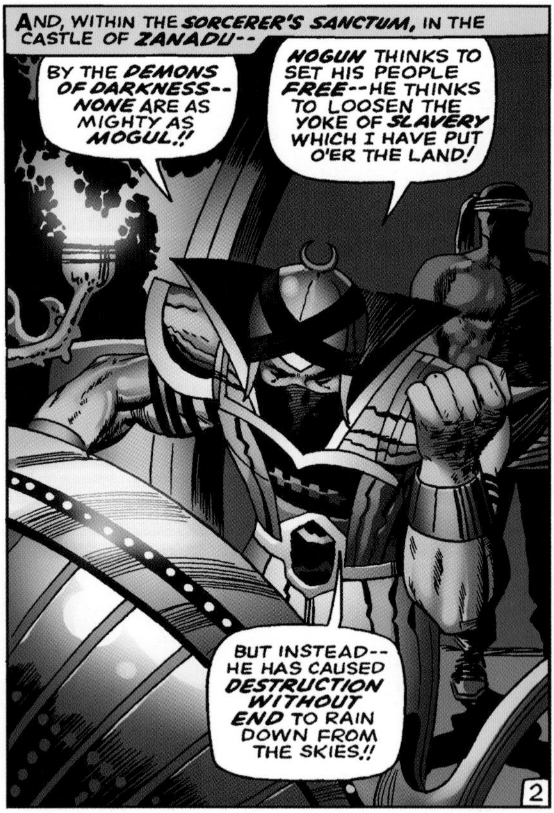
AND, WITHIN THE SORCERER'S SANCTUM, IN THE CASTLE OF ZANADU--
BY THE DEMONS OF DARKNESS--NONE ARE AS MIGHTY AS MOGUL!!
HOGUN THINKS TO SET HIS PEOPLE FREE--HE THINKS TO LOOSEN THE YOKE OF SLAVERY WHICH I HAVE PUT O'ER THE LAND!
BUT INSTEAD--HE HAS CAUSED DESTRUCTION WITHOUT END TO RAIN DOWN FROM THE SKIES!!
2

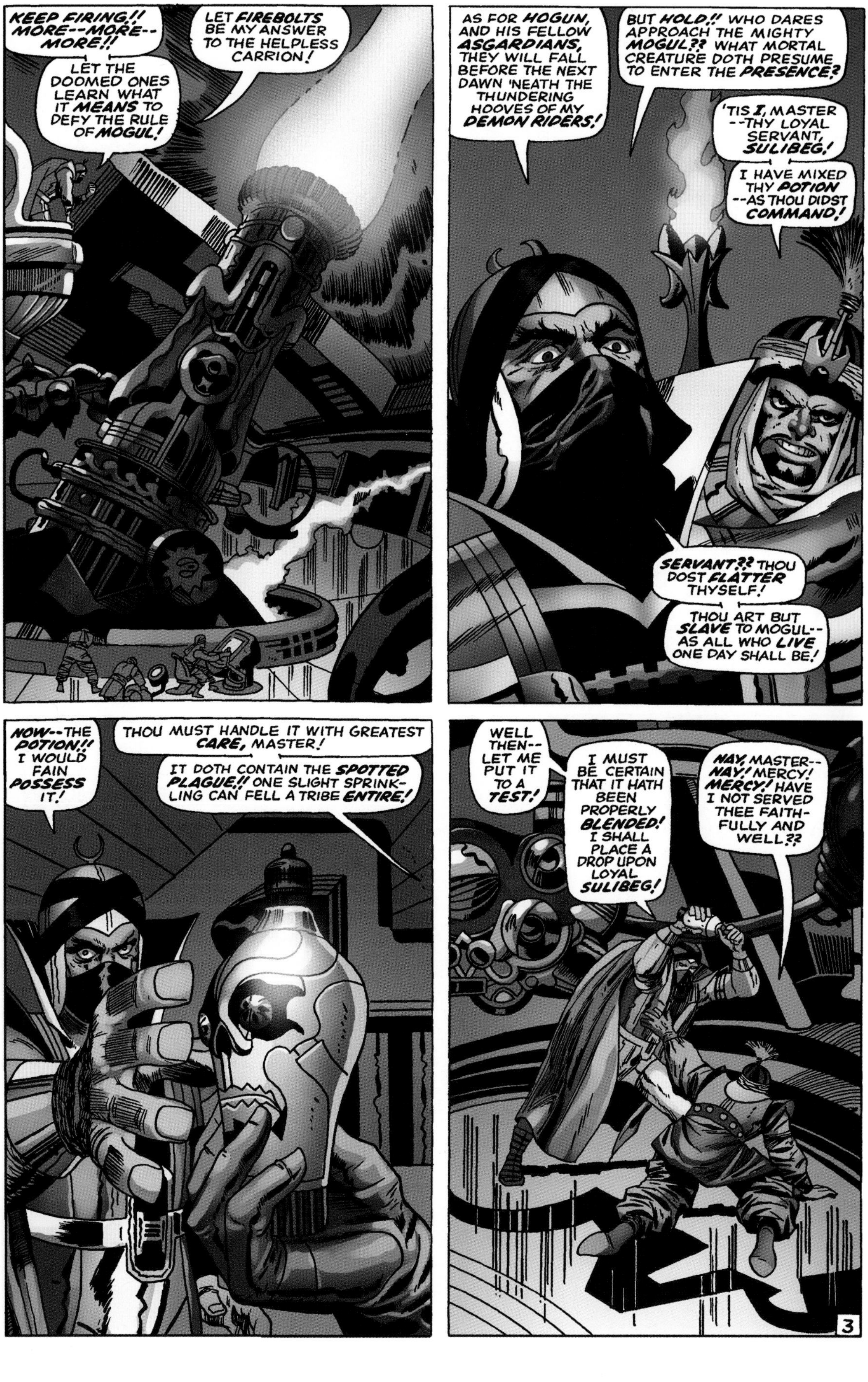
KEEP FIRING!! MORE--MORE--MORE!!
LET THE DOOMED ONES LEARN WHAT IT MEANS TO DEFY THE RULE OF MOGUL!
LET FIREBOLTS BE MY ANSWER TO THE HELPLESS CARRION!
AS FOR HOGUN, AND HIS FELLOW ASGARDIANS, THEY WILL FALL BEFORE THE NEXT DAWN 'NEATH THE THUNDERING HOOVES OF MY DEMON RIDERS!
BUT HOLD!! WHO DARES APPROACH THE MIGHTY MOGUL?? WHAT MORTAL CREATURE DOTH PRESUME TO ENTER THE PRESENCE?
'TIS I, MASTER --THY LOYAL SERVANT, SULIBEG!
I HAVE MIXED THY POTION --AS THOU DIDST COMMAND!
SERVANT?? THOU DOST FLATTER THYSELF!
THOU ART BUT SLAVE TO MOGUL-- AS ALL WHO LIVE ONE DAY SHALL BE!
NOW--THE POTION!! I WOULD FAIN POSSESS IT!
THOU MUST HANDLE IT WITH GREATEST CARE, MASTER!
IT DOTH CONTAIN THE SPOTTED PLAGUE!! ONE SLIGHT SPRINKLING CAN FELL A TRIBE ENTIRE!
WELL THEN-- LET ME PUT IT TO A TEST!
I MUST BE CERTAIN THAT IT HATH BEEN PROPERLY BLENDED! I SHALL PLACE A DROP UPON LOYAL SULIBEG!
NAY, MASTER-- NAY! MERCY! MERCY! HAVE I NOT SERVED THEE FAITHFULLY AND WELL??
3

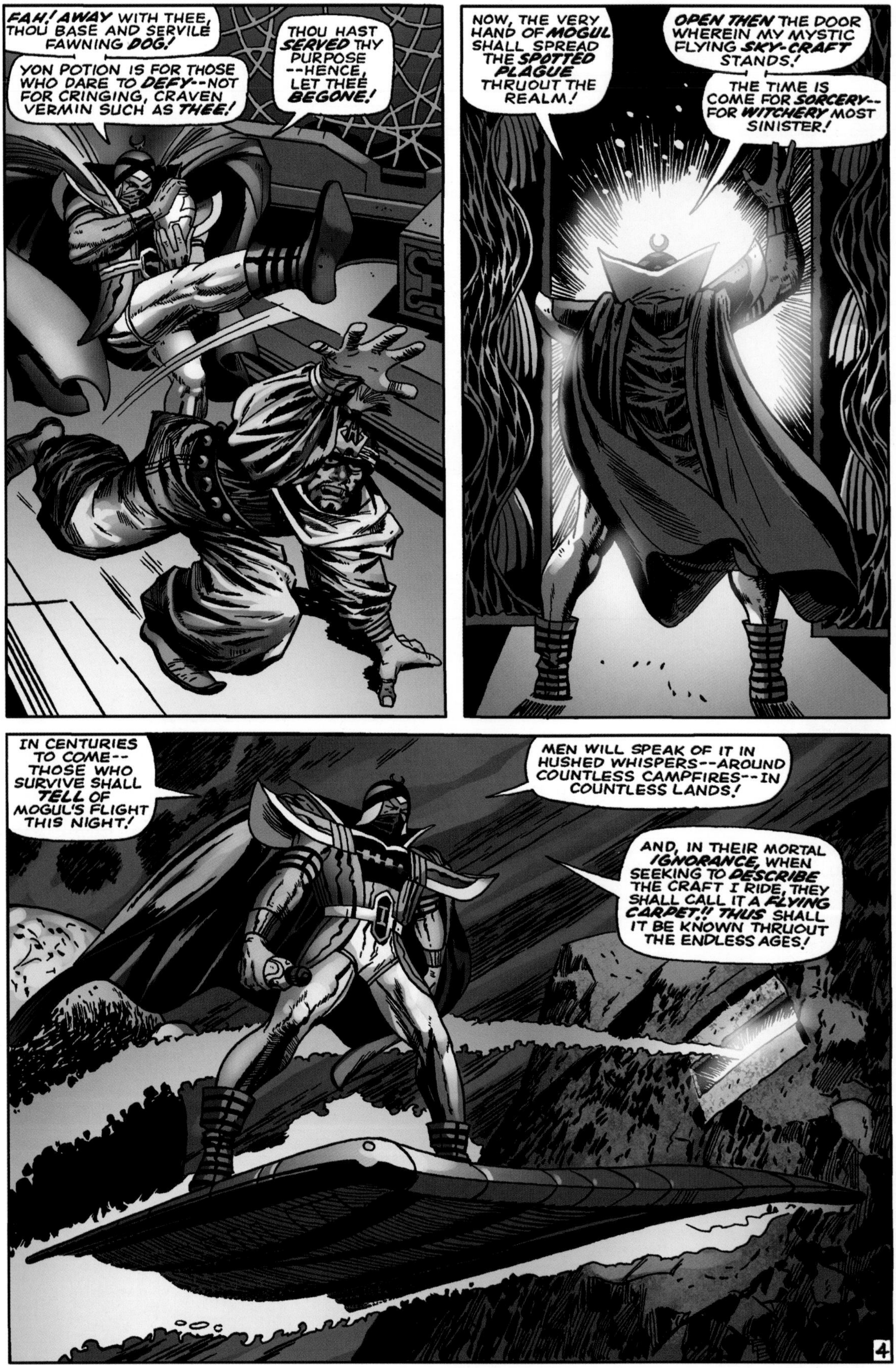
FAH! AWAY WITH THEE, THOU BASE AND SERVILE FAWNING DOG!
YON POTION IS FOR THOSE WHO DARE TO DEFY--NOT FOR CRINGING, CRAVEN VERMIN SUCH AS THEE!
THOU HAST SERVED THY PURPOSE --HENCE, LET THEE BEGONE!
NOW, THE VERY HAND OF MOGUL SHALL SPREAD THE SPOTTED PLAGUE THRUOUT THE REALM!
OPEN THEN THE DOOR WHEREIN MY MYSTIC FLYING SKY-CRAFT STANDS!
THE TIME IS COME FOR SORCERY-- FOR WITCHERY MOST SINISTER!
IN CENTURIES TO COME-- THOSE WHO SURVIVE SHALL TELL OF MOGUL'S FLIGHT THIS NIGHT!
MEN WILL SPEAK OF IT IN HUSHED WHISPERS--AROUND COUNTLESS CAMPFIRES--IN COUNTLESS LANDS!
AND, IN THEIR MORTAL IGNORANCE, WHEN SEEKING TO DESCRIBE THE CRAFT I RIDE, THEY SHALL CALL IT A FLYING CARPET!! THUS SHALL IT BE KNOWN THRUOUT THE ENDLESS AGES!
4

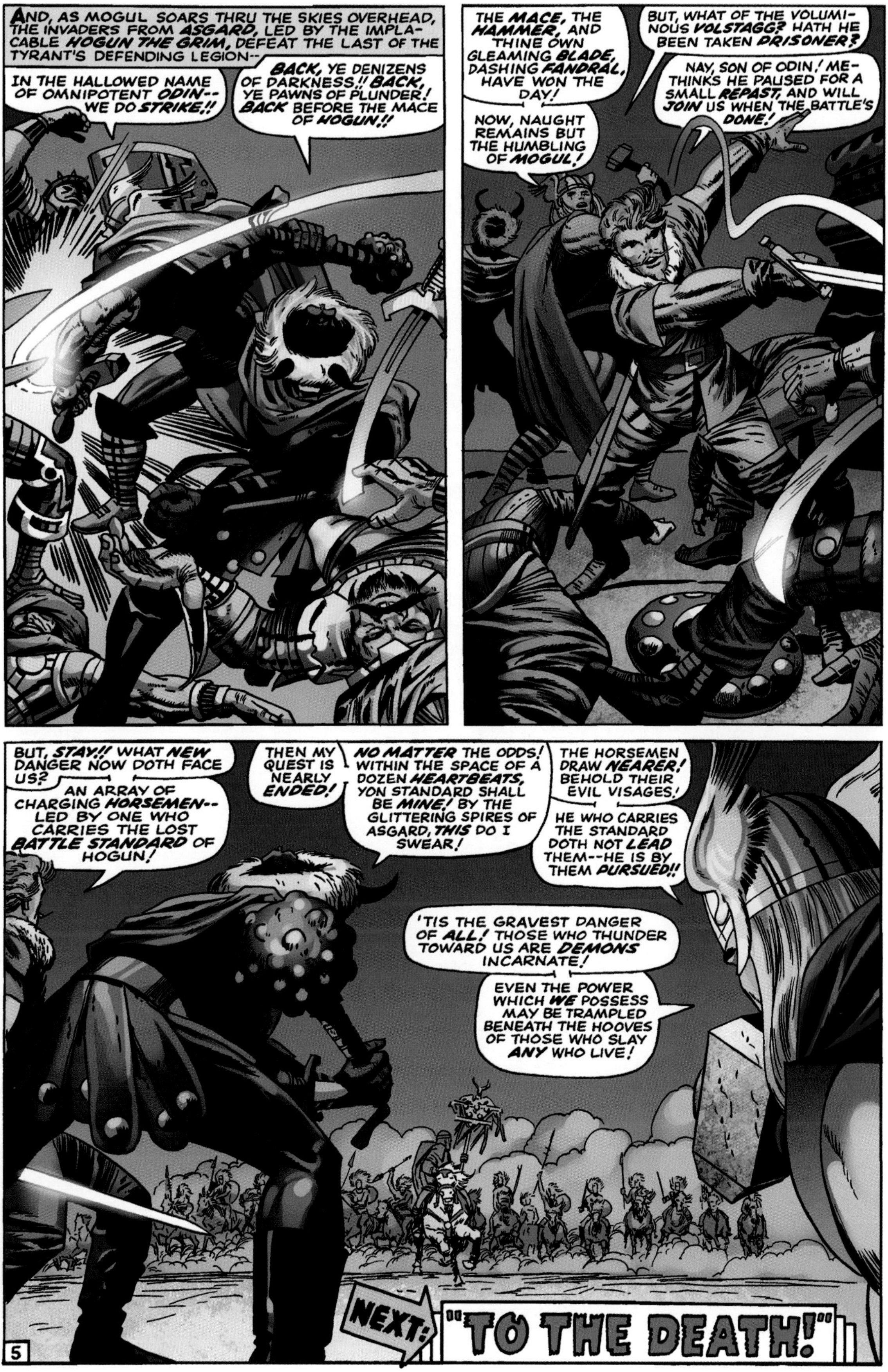
AND, AS MOGUL SOARS THRU THE SKIES OVERHEAD, THE INVADERS FROM ASGARD, LED BY THE IMPLACABLE HOGUN THE GRIM, DEFEAT THE LAST OF THE TYRANT'S DEFENDING LEGION--
IN THE HALLOWED NAME OF OMNIPOTENT ODIN-- WE DO STRIKE!!
BACK, YE DENIZENS OF DARKNESS!! BACK, YE PAWNS OF PLUNDER! BACK BEFORE THE MACE OF HOGUN!!
THE MACE, THE HAMMER, AND THINE OWN GLEAMING BLADE, DASHING FANDRAL, HAVE WON THE DAY!
NOW, NAUGHT REMAINS BUT THE HUMBLING OF MOGUL!
BUT, WHAT OF THE VOLUMINOUS VOLSTAGG? HATH HE BEEN TAKEN PRISONER?
NAY, SON OF ODIN! METHINKS HE PAUSED FOR A SMALL REPAST, AND WILL JOIN US WHEN THE BATTLE'S DONE!
BUT, STAY!! WHAT NEW DANGER NOW DOTH FACE US?
AN ARRAY OF CHARGING HORSEMEN-- LED BY ONE WHO CARRIES THE LOST BATTLE STANDARD OF HOGUN!
THEN MY QUEST IS NEARLY ENDED!
NO MATTER THE ODDS! WITHIN THE SPACE OF A DOZEN HEARTBEATS, YON STANDARD SHALL BE MINE! BY THE GLITTERING SPIRES OF ASGARD, THIS DO I SWEAR!
THE HORSEMEN DRAW NEARER! BEHOLD THEIR EVIL VISAGES!
HE WHO CARRIES THE STANDARD DOTH NOT LEAD THEM--HE IS BY THEM PURSUED!!
'TIS THE GRAVEST DANGER OF ALL! THOSE WHO THUNDER TOWARD US ARE DEMONS INCARNATE!
EVEN THE POWER WHICH WE POSSESS MAY BE TRAMPLED BENEATH THE HOOVES OF THOSE WHO SLAY ANY WHO LIVE!
NEXT: "TO THE DEATH!"
5

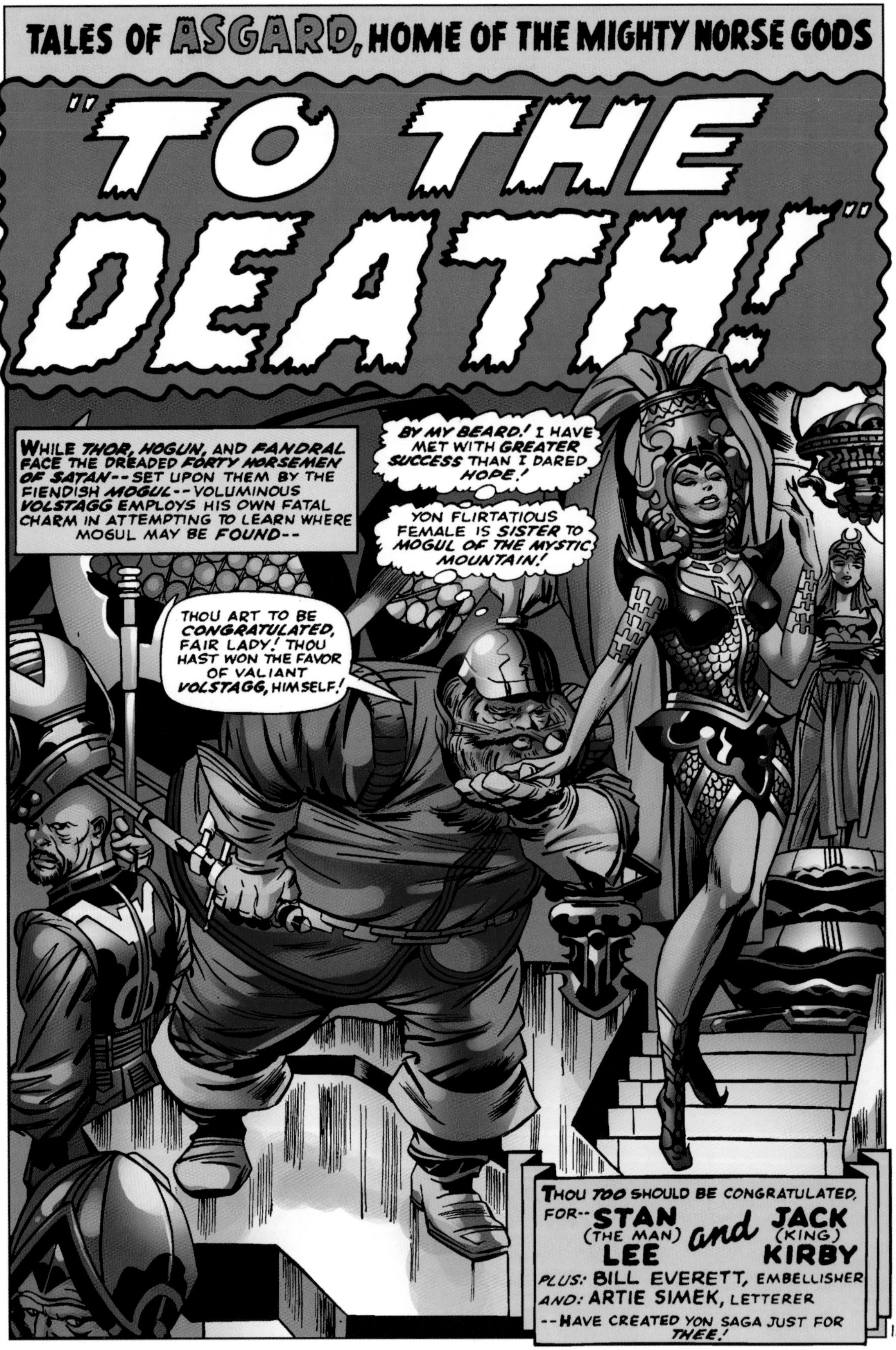
TALES OF ASGARD, HOME OF THE MIGHTY NORSE GODS
"TO THE DEATH!"
WHILE THOR, HOGUN, AND FANDRAL FACE THE DREADED FORTY HORSEMEN OF SATAN--SET UPON THEM BY THE FIENDISH MOGUL--VOLUMINOUS VOLSTAGG EMPLOYS HIS OWN FATAL CHARM IN ATTEMPTING TO LEARN WHERE MOGUL MAY BE FOUND--
BY MY BEARD! I HAVE MET WITH GREATER SUCCESS THAN I DARED HOPE!
YON FLIRTATIOUS FEMALE IS SISTER TO MOGUL OF THE MYSTIC MOUNTAIN!
THOU ART TO BE CONGRATULATED, FAIR LADY! THOU HAST WON THE FAVOR OF VALIANT VOLSTAGG, HIMSELF!
THOU TOO SHOULD BE CONGRATULATED, FOR--STAN (THE MAN) LEE and JACK (KING) KIRBY
PLUS: BILL EVERETT, EMBELLISHER
AND: ARTIE SIMEK, LETTERER
--HAVE CREATED YON SAGA JUST FOR THEE!
1.

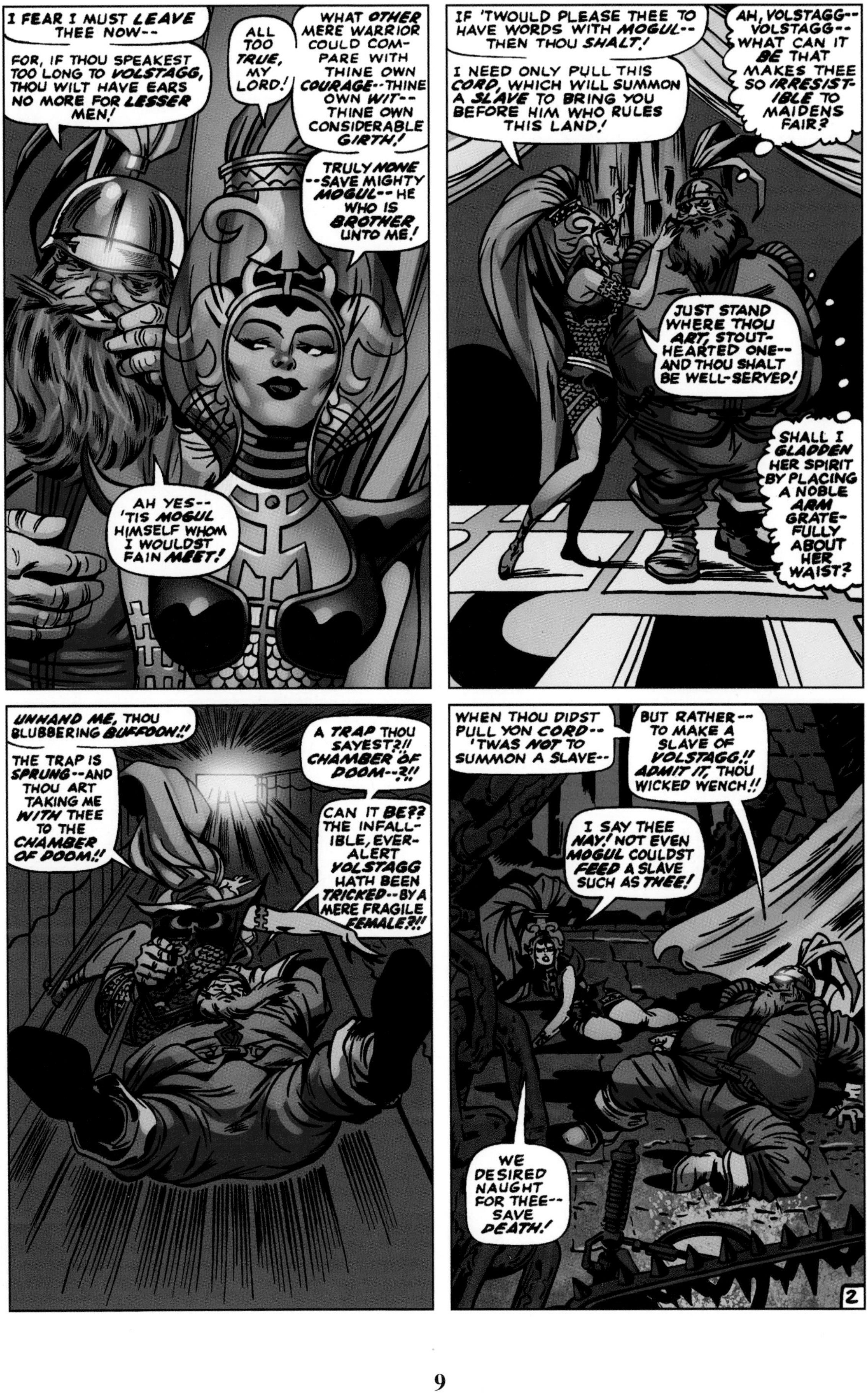

I FEAR I MUST LEAVE THEE NOW--
FOR, IF THOU SPEAKEST TOO LONG TO VOLSTAGG, THOU WILT HAVE EARS NO MORE FOR LESSER MEN!
ALL TOO TRUE, MY LORD!
WHAT OTHER MERE WARRIOR COULD COMPARE WITH THINE OWN COURAGE--THINE OWN WIT--THINE OWN CONSIDERABLE GIRTH!
TRULY NONE--SAVE MIGHTY MOGUL--HE WHO IS BROTHER UNTO ME!
AH YES--'TIS MOGUL HIMSELF WHOM I WOULDST FAIN MEET!
IF 'TWOULD PLEASE THEE TO HAVE WORDS WITH MOGUL--THEN THOU SHALT!
I NEED ONLY PULL THIS CORD, WHICH WILL SUMMON A SLAVE TO BRING YOU BEFORE HIM WHO RULES THIS LAND!
AH, VOLSTAGG--VOLSTAGG--WHAT CAN IT BE THAT MAKES THEE SO IRRESISTIBLE TO MAIDENS FAIR?
JUST STAND WHERE THOU ART, STOUT-HEARTED ONE--AND THOU SHALT BE WELL-SERVED!
SHALL I GLADDEN HER SPIRIT BY PLACING A NOBLE ARM GRATEFULLY ABOUT HER WAIST?
UNHAND ME, THOU BLUBBERING BUFFOON!!
THE TRAP IS SPRUNG--AND THOU ART TAKING ME WITH THEE TO THE CHAMBER OF DOOM!!
A TRAP THOU SAYEST?!! CHAMBER OF DOOM--?!!
CAN IT BE?? THE INFALLIBLE, EVER-ALERT VOLSTAGG HATH BEEN TRICKED--BY A MERE FRAGILE FEMALE?!!
WHEN THOU DIDST PULL YON CORD--'TWAS NOT TO SUMMON A SLAVE--
BUT RATHER--TO MAKE A SLAVE OF VOLSTAGG!! ADMIT IT, THOU WICKED WENCH!!
I SAY THEE NAY! NOT EVEN MOGUL COULDST FEED A SLAVE SUCH AS THEE!
WE DESIRED NAUGHT FOR THEE--SAVE DEATH!
2

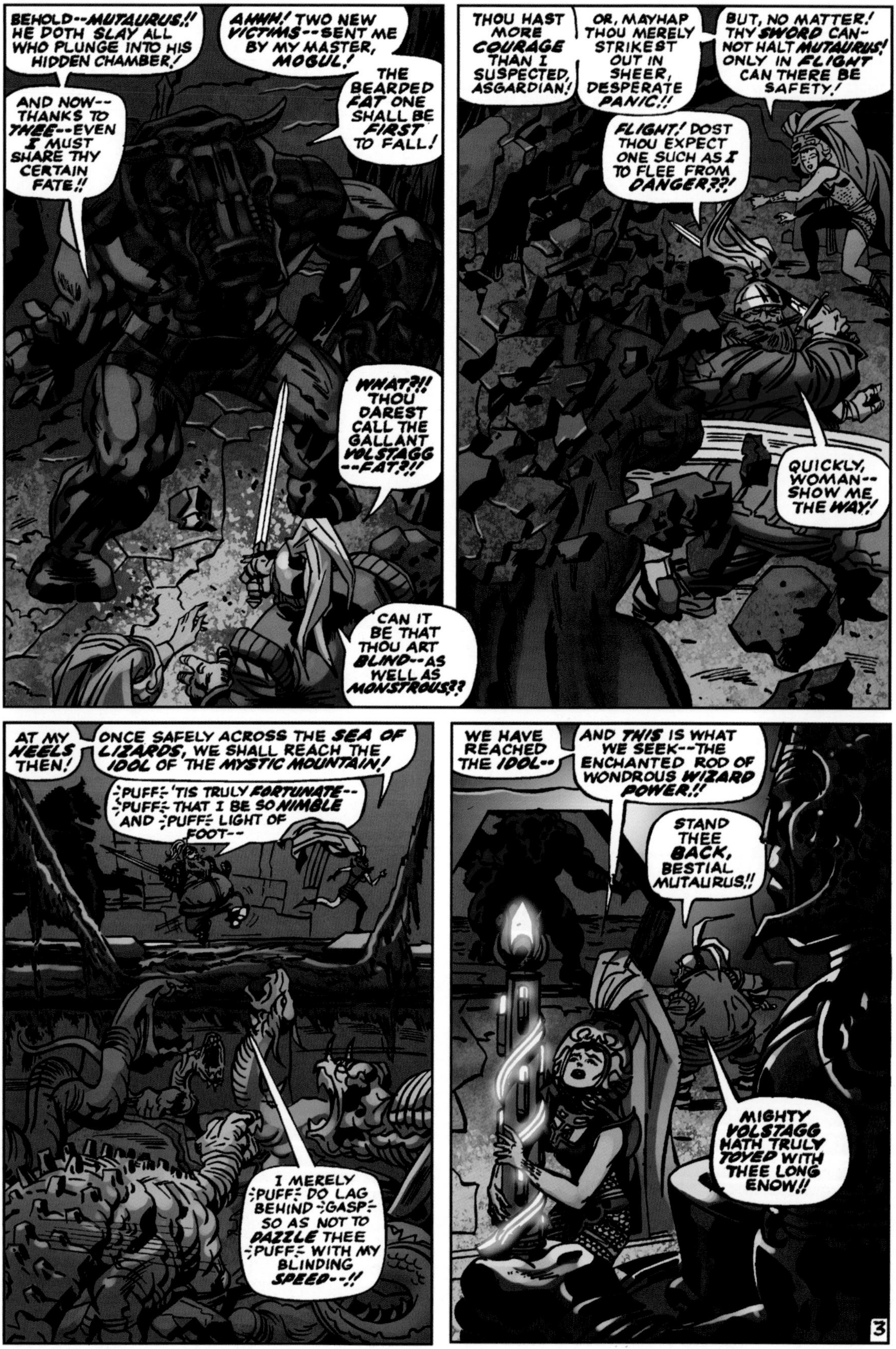
BEHOLD--MUTAURUS!! HE DOTH SLAY ALL WHO PLUNGE INTO HIS HIDDEN CHAMBER!
AND NOW--THANKS TO THEE--EVEN I MUST SHARE THY CERTAIN FATE!!
AHHH! TWO NEW VICTIMS--SENT ME BY MY MASTER, MOGUL!
THE BEARDED FAT ONE SHALL BE FIRST TO FALL!
WHAT?!! THOU DAREST CALL THE GALLANT VOLSTAGG--FAT?!!
CAN IT BE THAT THOU ART BLIND--AS WELL AS MONSTROUS??
THOU HAST MORE COURAGE THAN I SUSPECTED, ASGARDIAN!
OR, MAYHAP THOU MERELY STRIKEST OUT IN SHEER, DESPERATE PANIC!!
BUT, NO MATTER! THY SWORD CANNOT HALT MUTAURUS! ONLY IN FLIGHT CAN THERE BE SAFETY!
FLIGHT! DOST THOU EXPECT ONE SUCH AS I TO FLEE FROM DANGER??!
QUICKLY, WOMAN--SHOW ME THE WAY!
AT MY HEELS THEN!
ONCE SAFELY ACROSS THE SEA OF LIZARDS, WE SHALL REACH THE IDOL OF THE MYSTIC MOUNTAIN!
-PUFF- 'TIS TRULY FORTUNATE-- -PUFF- THAT I BE SO NIMBLE AND -PUFF- LIGHT OF FOOT--
I MERELY -PUFF- DO LAG BEHIND -GASP- SO AS NOT TO DAZZLE THEE -PUFF- WITH MY BLINDING SPEED--!!
WE HAVE REACHED THE IDOL--
AND THIS IS WHAT WE SEEK--THE ENCHANTED ROD OF WONDROUS WIZARD POWER!!
STAND THEE BACK, BESTIAL MUTAURUS!!
MIGHTY VOLSTAGG HATH TRULY TOYED WITH THEE LONG ENOW!!
3

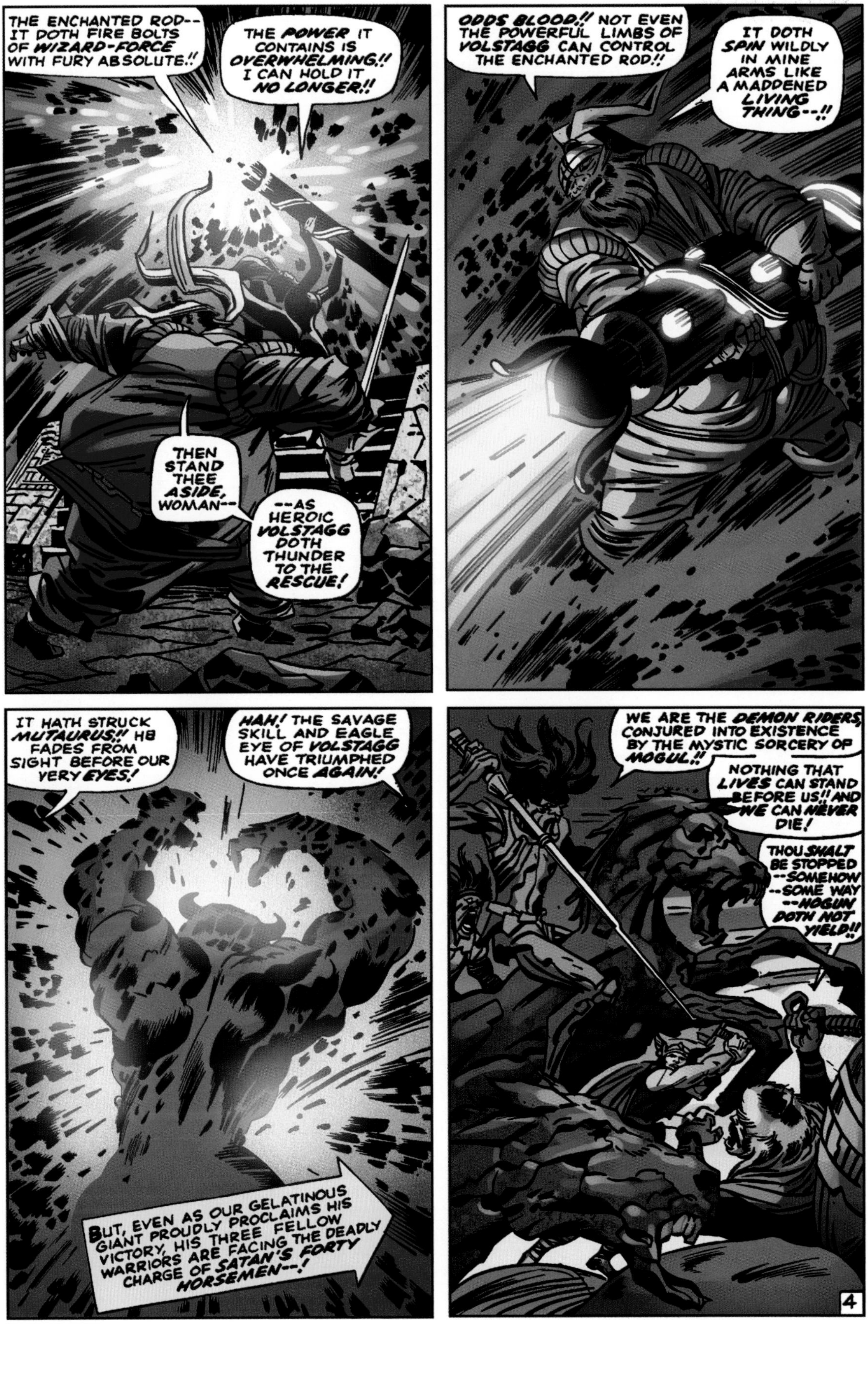
THE ENCHANTED ROD-- IT DOTH FIRE BOLTS OF WIZARD-FORCE WITH FURY ABSOLUTE!!
THE POWER IT CONTAINS IS OVERWHELMING!! I CAN HOLD IT NO LONGER!!
THEN STAND THEE ASIDE, WOMAN--
--AS HEROIC VOLSTAGG DOTH THUNDER TO THE RESCUE!
ODDS BLOOD!! NOT EVEN THE POWERFUL LIMBS OF VOLSTAGG CAN CONTROL THE ENCHANTED ROD!!
IT DOTH SPIN WILDLY IN MINE ARMS LIKE A MADDENED LIVING THING--!!
IT HATH STRUCK MUTAURUS!! HE FADES FROM SIGHT BEFORE OUR VERY EYES!
HAH! THE SAVAGE SKILL AND EAGLE EYE OF VOLSTAGG HAVE TRIUMPHED ONCE AGAIN!
BUT, EVEN AS OUR GELATINOUS GIANT PROUDLY PROCLAIMS HIS VICTORY, HIS THREE FELLOW WARRIORS ARE FACING THE DEADLY CHARGE OF SATAN'S FORTY HORSEMEN--!
WE ARE THE DEMON RIDERS, CONJURED INTO EXISTENCE BY THE MYSTIC SORCERY OF MOGUL!!
NOTHING THAT LIVES CAN STAND BEFORE US!! AND WE CAN NEVER DIE!
THOU SHALT BE STOPPED --SOMEHOW --SOME WAY --HOGUN DOTH NOT YIELD!!
4

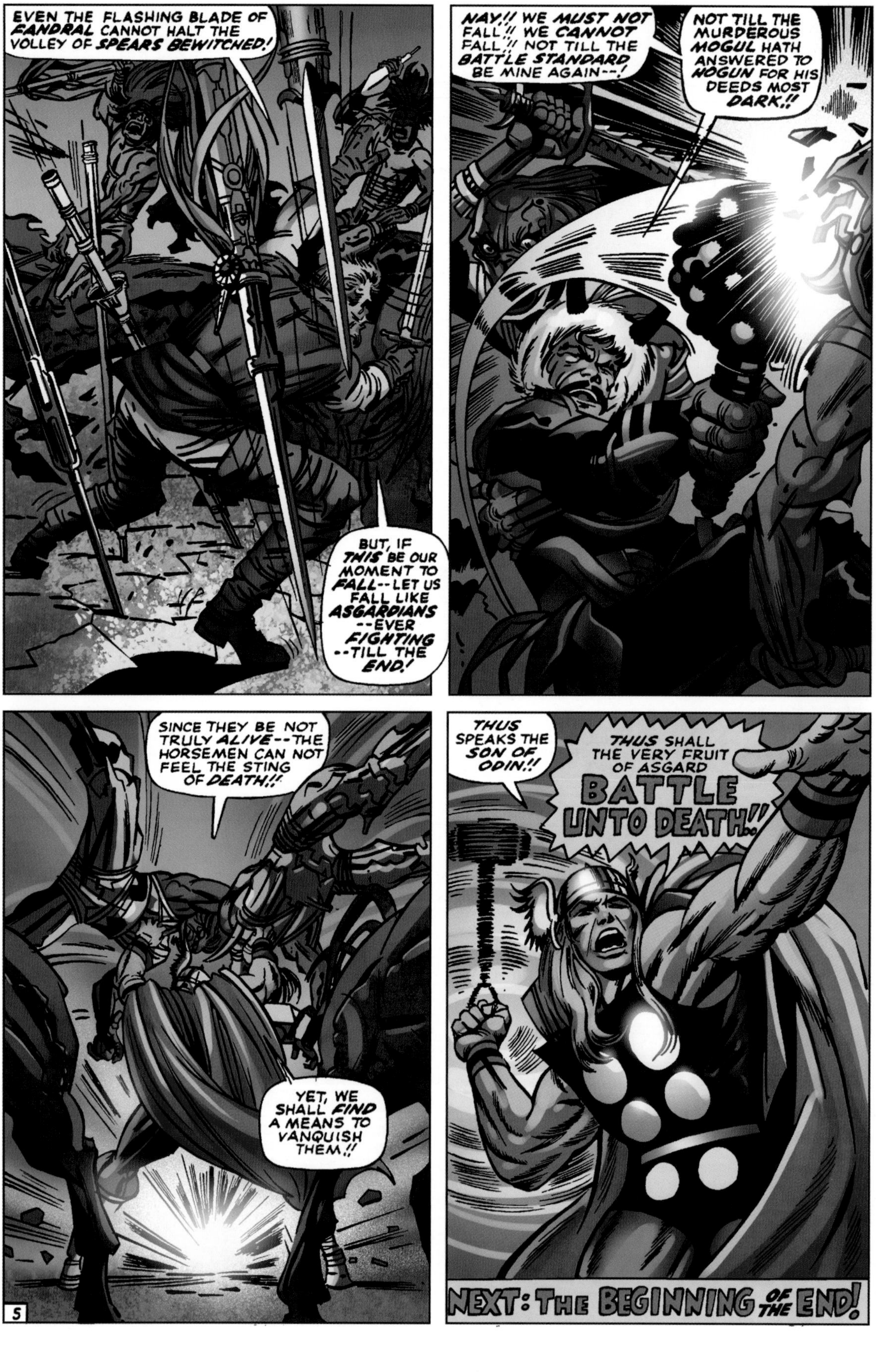
EVEN THE FLASHING BLADE OF FANDRAL CANNOT HALT THE VOLLEY OF SPEARS BEWITCHED!
BUT, IF THIS BE OUR MOMENT TO FALL--LET US FALL LIKE ASGARDIANS --EVER FIGHTING --TILL THE END!
NAY!! WE MUST NOT FALL!! WE CANNOT FALL!! NOT TILL THE BATTLE STANDARD BE MINE AGAIN--!
NOT TILL THE MURDEROUS MOGUL HATH ANSWERED TO HOGUN FOR HIS DEEDS MOST DARK!!
SINCE THEY BE NOT TRULY ALIVE--THE HORSEMEN CAN NOT FEEL THE STING OF DEATH!!
YET, WE SHALL FIND A MEANS TO VANQUISH THEM!!
5
THUS SPEAKS THE SON OF ODIN!!
THUS SHALL THE VERY FRUIT OF ASGARD BATTLE UNTO DEATH!!
NEXT: THE BEGINNING OF THE END!

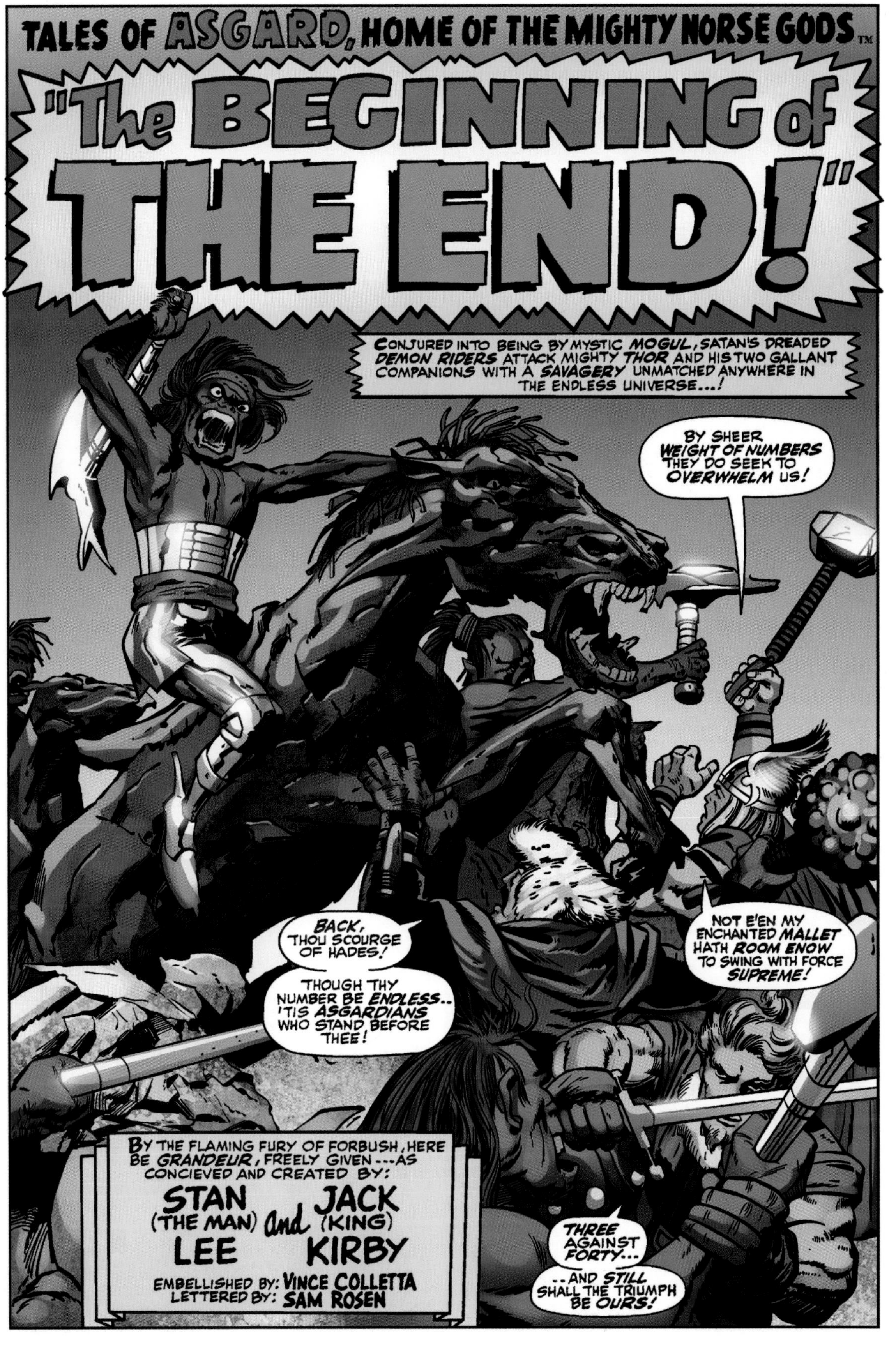

TALES OF ASGARD, HOME OF THE MIGHTY NORSE GODS™
"The BEGINNING of THE END!"
CONJURED INTO BEING BY MYSTIC MOGUL, SATAN'S DREADED DEMON RIDERS ATTACK MIGHTY THOR AND HIS TWO GALLANT COMPANIONS WITH A SAVAGERY UNMATCHED ANYWHERE IN THE ENDLESS UNIVERSE...!
BY SHEER WEIGHT OF NUMBERS THEY DO SEEK TO OVERWHELM US!
BACK, THOU SCOURGE OF HADES!
THOUGH THY NUMBER BE ENDLESS.. 'TIS ASGARDIANS WHO STAND BEFORE THEE!
NOT E'EN MY ENCHANTED MALLET HATH ROOM ENOW TO SWING WITH FORCE SUPREME!
BY THE FLAMING FURY OF FORBUSH, HERE BE GRANDEUR, FREELY GIVEN---AS CONCIEVED AND CREATED BY:
STAN (THE MAN) LEE and JACK (KING) KIRBY
EMBELLISHED BY: VINCE COLLETTA
LETTERED BY: SAM ROSEN
THREE AGAINST FORTY...
..AND STILL SHALL THE TRIUMPH BE OURS!

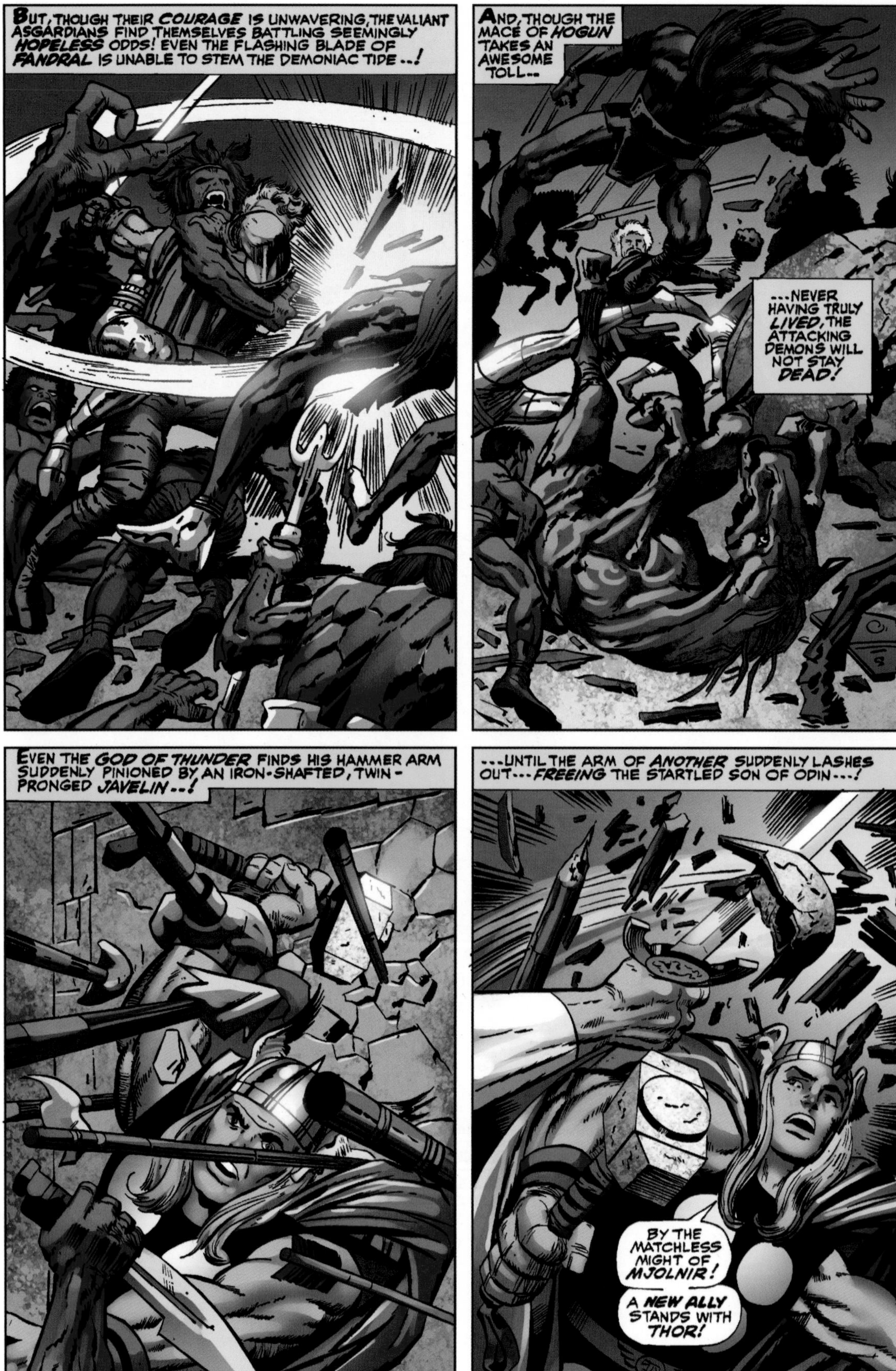
BUT, THOUGH THEIR COURAGE IS UNWAVERING, THE VALIANT ASGARDIANS FIND THEMSELVES BATTLING SEEMINGLY HOPELESS ODDS! EVEN THE FLASHING BLADE OF FANDRAL IS UNABLE TO STEM THE DEMONIAC TIDE--!
AND, THOUGH THE MACE OF HOGUN TAKES AN AWESOME TOLL--
---NEVER HAVING TRULY LIVED, THE ATTACKING DEMONS WILL NOT STAY DEAD!
EVEN THE GOD OF THUNDER FINDS HIS HAMMER ARM SUDDENLY PINIONED BY AN IRON-SHAFTED, TWIN-PRONGED JAVELIN--!
---UNTIL THE ARM OF ANOTHER SUDDENLY LASHES OUT---FREEING THE STARTLED SON OF ODIN---!
BY THE MATCHLESS MIGHT OF MJOLNIR!
A NEW ALLY STANDS WITH THOR!
2.

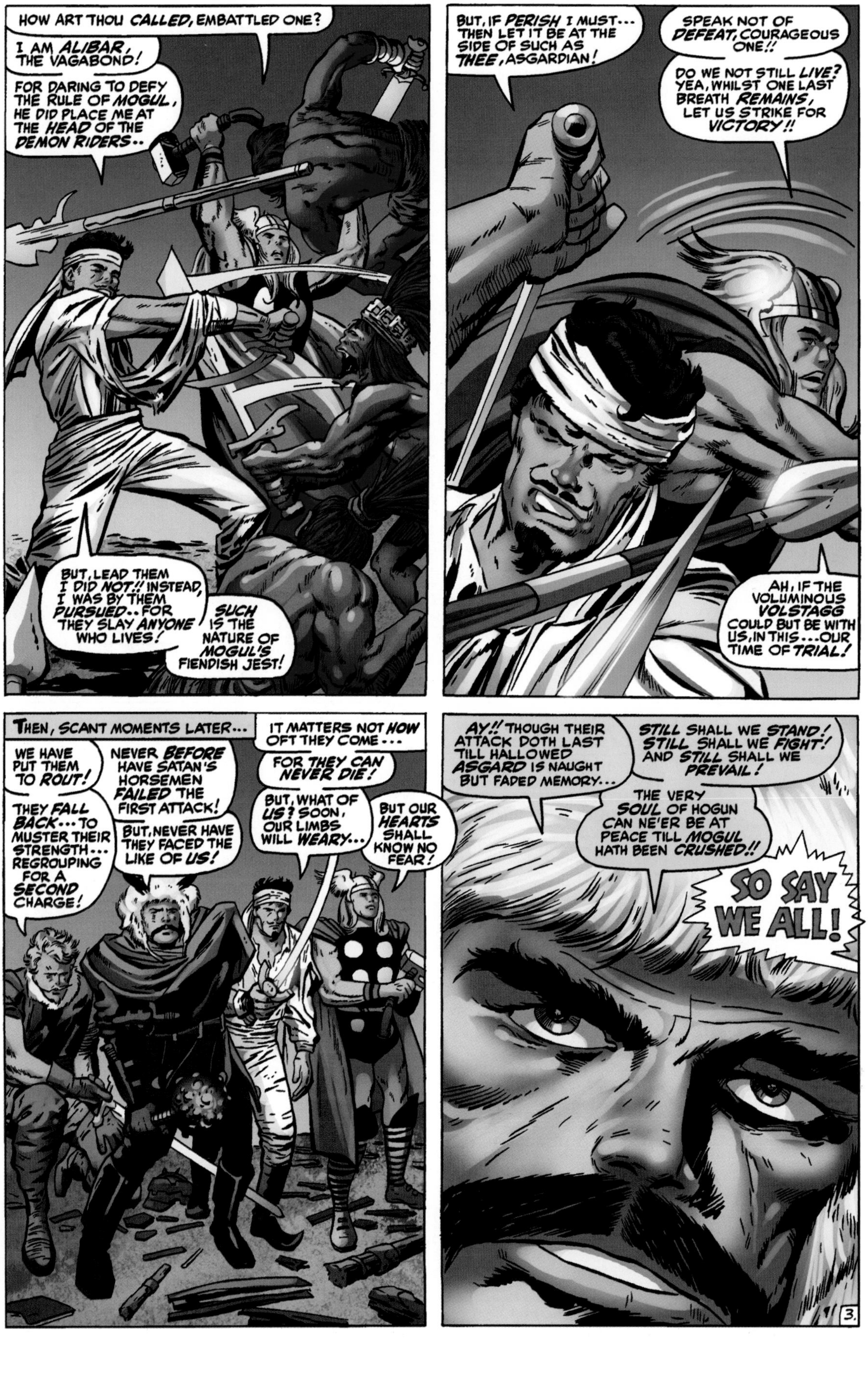

HOW ART THOU CALLED, EMBATTLED ONE?
I AM ALIBAR, THE VAGABOND!
FOR DARING TO DEFY THE RULE OF MOGUL, HE DID PLACE ME AT THE HEAD OF THE DEMON RIDERS..
BUT, LEAD THEM I DID NOT!! INSTEAD, I WAS BY THEM PURSUED..FOR THEY SLAY ANYONE WHO LIVES!
SUCH IS THE NATURE OF MOGUL'S FIENDISH JEST!
BUT, IF PERISH I MUST... THEN LET IT BE AT THE SIDE OF SUCH AS THEE, ASGARDIAN!
SPEAK NOT OF DEFEAT, COURAGEOUS ONE!!
DO WE NOT STILL LIVE? YEA, WHILST ONE LAST BREATH REMAINS, LET US STRIKE FOR VICTORY!!
AH, IF THE VOLUMINOUS VOLSTAGG COULD BUT BE WITH US, IN THIS...OUR TIME OF TRIAL!
THEN, SCANT MOMENTS LATER...
WE HAVE PUT THEM TO ROUT!
NEVER BEFORE HAVE SATAN'S HORSEMEN FAILED THE FIRST ATTACK!
THEY FALL BACK...TO MUSTER THEIR STRENGTH... REGROUPING FOR A SECOND CHARGE!
BUT, NEVER HAVE THEY FACED THE LIKE OF US!
IT MATTERS NOT HOW OFT THEY COME...
FOR THEY CAN NEVER DIE!
BUT, WHAT OF US? SOON, OUR LIMBS WILL WEARY...
BUT OUR HEARTS SHALL KNOW NO FEAR!
AY!! THOUGH THEIR ATTACK DOTH LAST TILL HALLOWED ASGARD IS NAUGHT BUT FADED MEMORY...
STILL SHALL WE STAND! STILL SHALL WE FIGHT! AND STILL SHALL WE PREVAIL!
THE VERY SOUL OF HOGUN CAN NE'ER BE AT PEACE TILL MOGUL HATH BEEN CRUSHED!!
SO SAY WE ALL!
3.

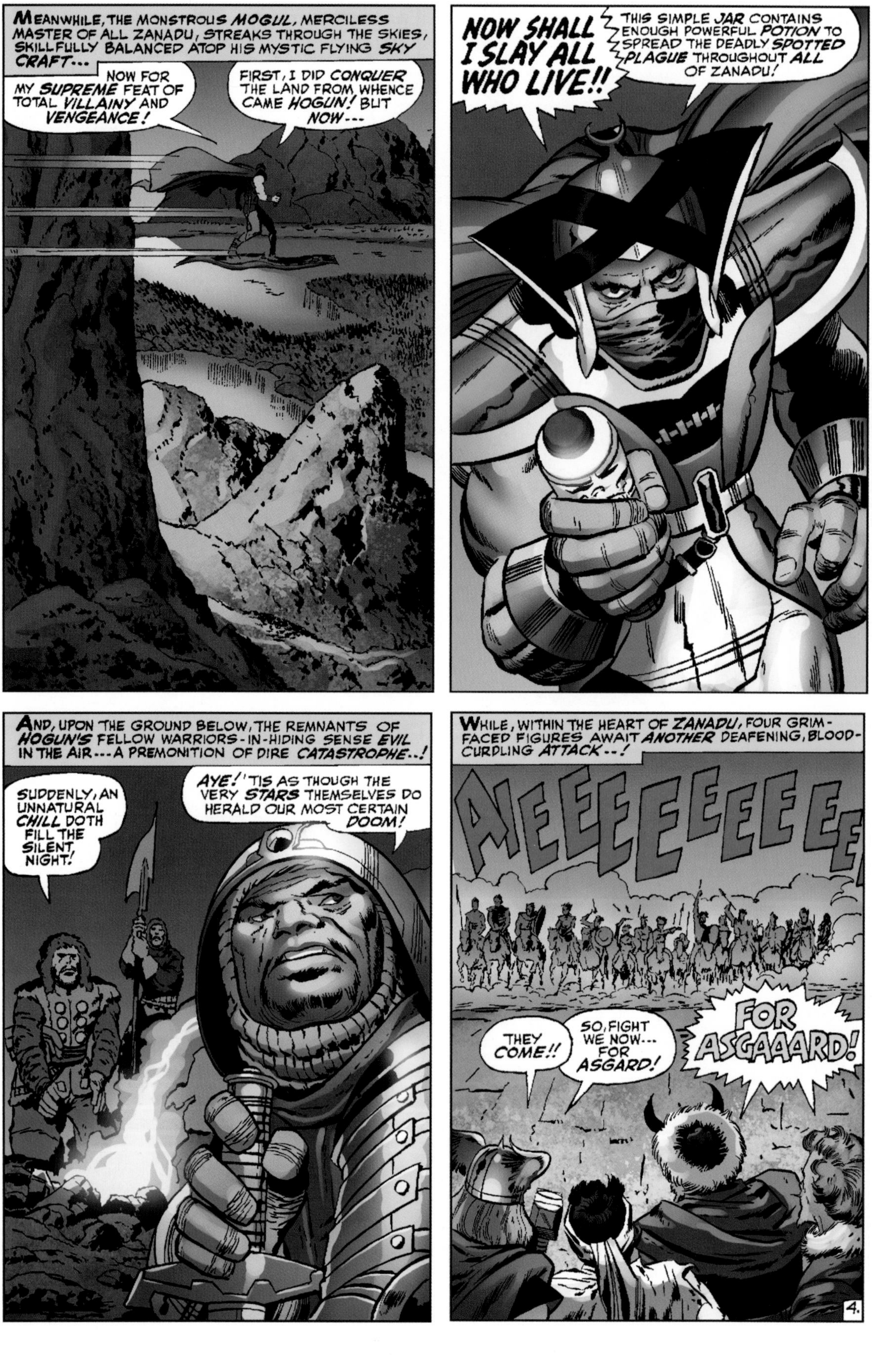
MEANWHILE, THE MONSTROUS MOGUL, MERCILESS MASTER OF ALL ZANADU, STREAKS THROUGH THE SKIES, SKILLFULLY BALANCED ATOP HIS MYSTIC FLYING SKY CRAFT...
NOW FOR MY SUPREME FEAT OF TOTAL VILLAINY AND VENGEANCE!
FIRST, I DID CONQUER THE LAND FROM WHENCE CAME HOGUN! BUT NOW---
NOW SHALL I SLAY ALL WHO LIVE!!
THIS SIMPLE JAR CONTAINS ENOUGH POWERFUL POTION TO SPREAD THE DEADLY SPOTTED PLAGUE THROUGHOUT ALL OF ZANADU!
AND, UPON THE GROUND BELOW, THE REMNANTS OF HOGUN'S FELLOW WARRIORS-IN-HIDING SENSE EVIL IN THE AIR---A PREMONITION OF DIRE CATASTROPHE..!
SUDDENLY, AN UNNATURAL CHILL DOTH FILL THE SILENT NIGHT!
AYE! 'TIS AS THOUGH THE VERY STARS THEMSELVES DO HERALD OUR MOST CERTAIN DOOM!
WHILE, WITHIN THE HEART OF ZANADU, FOUR GRIM-FACED FIGURES AWAIT ANOTHER DEAFENING, BLOOD-CURDLING ATTACK--!
AIEEEEEEEEEE
THEY COME!!
SO, FIGHT WE NOW--- FOR ASGARD!
FOR ASGAAARD!
4.

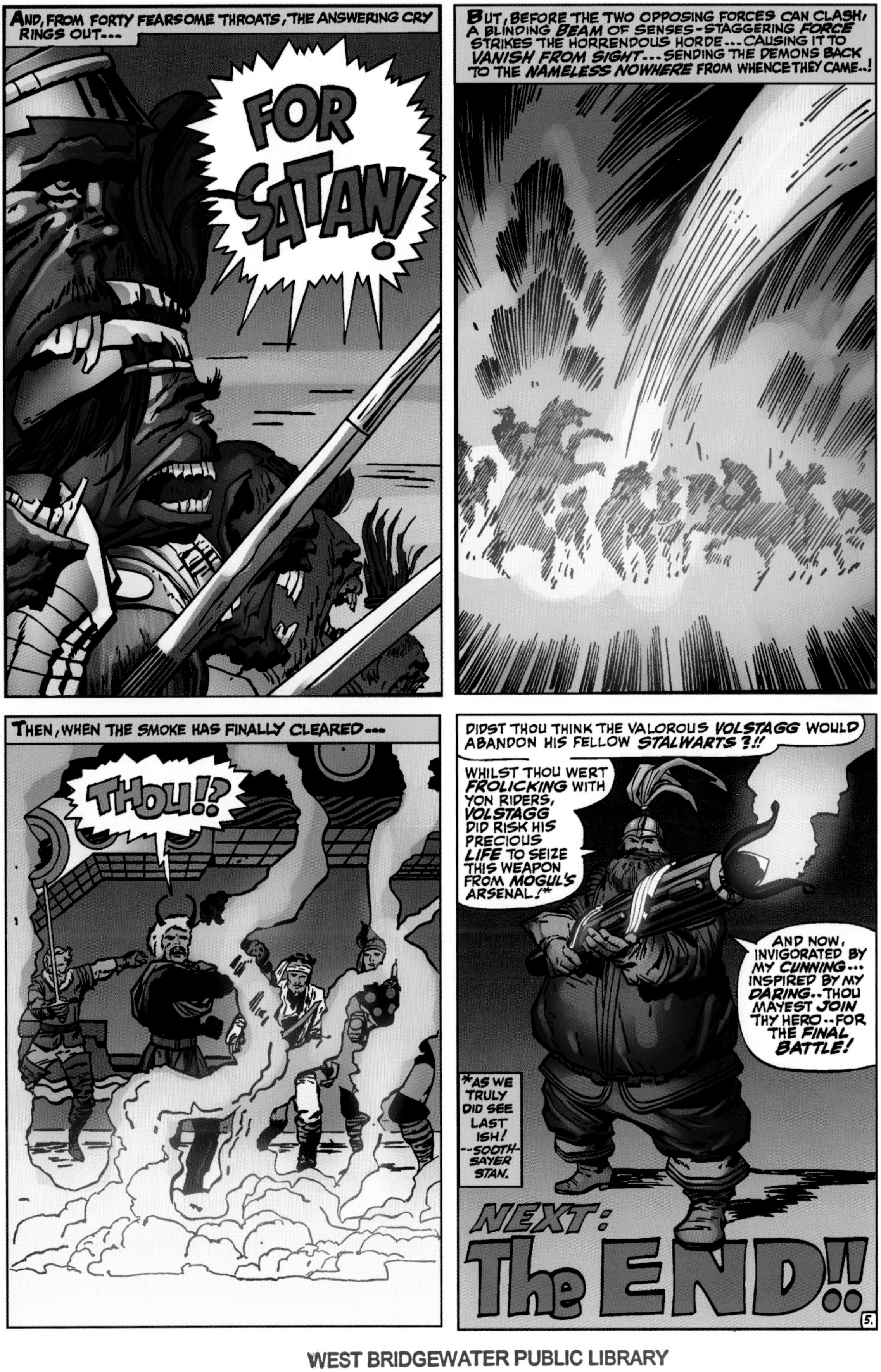

AND, FROM FORTY FEARSOME THROATS, THE ANSWERING CRY RINGS OUT...
FOR SATAN!
BUT, BEFORE THE TWO OPPOSING FORCES CAN CLASH, A BLINDING BEAM OF SENSES-STAGGERING FORCE STRIKES THE HORRENDOUS HORDE... CAUSING IT TO VANISH FROM SIGHT... SENDING THE DEMONS BACK TO THE NAMELESS NOWHERE FROM WHENCE THEY CAME..!
THEN, WHEN THE SMOKE HAS FINALLY CLEARED...
THOU!?
DIDST THOU THINK THE VALOROUS VOLSTAGG WOULD ABANDON HIS FELLOW STALWARTS?!!
WHILST THOU WERT FROLICKING WITH YON RIDERS, VOLSTAGG DID RISK HIS PRECIOUS LIFE TO SEIZE THIS WEAPON FROM MOGUL'S ARSENAL!*
AND NOW, INVIGORATED BY MY CUNNING... INSPIRED BY MY DARING.. THOU MAYEST JOIN THY HERO.. FOR THE FINAL BATTLE!
*AS WE TRULY DID SEE LAST ISH! --SOOTH-SAYER STAN.
NEXT: The END!!
5.

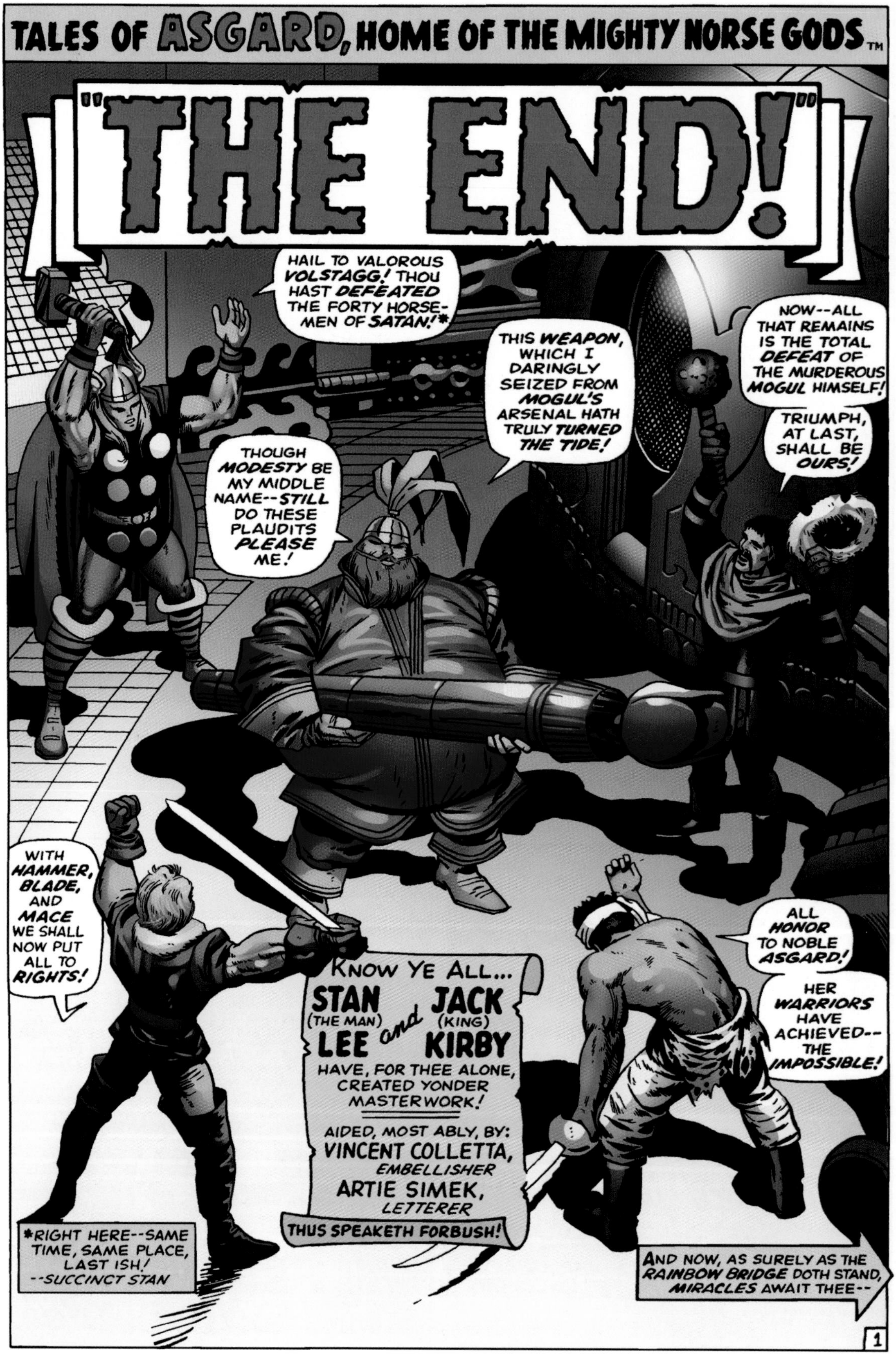

TALES OF ASGARD, HOME OF THE MIGHTY NORSE GODS ™
"THE END!"
HAIL TO VALOROUS VOLSTAGG! THOU HAST DEFEATED THE FORTY HORSEMEN OF SATAN!*
THIS WEAPON, WHICH I DARINGLY SEIZED FROM MOGUL'S ARSENAL HATH TRULY TURNED THE TIDE!
NOW--ALL THAT REMAINS IS THE TOTAL DEFEAT OF THE MURDEROUS MOGUL HIMSELF!
TRIUMPH, AT LAST, SHALL BE OURS!
THOUGH MODESTY BE MY MIDDLE NAME--STILL DO THESE PLAUDITS PLEASE ME.!
WITH HAMMER, BLADE, AND MACE WE SHALL NOW PUT ALL TO RIGHTS!
ALL HONOR TO NOBLE ASGARD!
HER WARRIORS HAVE ACHIEVED-- THE IMPOSSIBLE!
KNOW YE ALL... STAN (THE MAN) LEE and JACK (KING) KIRBY HAVE, FOR THEE ALONE, CREATED YONDER MASTERWORK!
AIDED, MOST ABLY, BY: VINCENT COLLETTA, EMBELLISHER ARTIE SIMEK, LETTERER
THUS SPEAKETH FORBUSH!
*RIGHT HERE--SAME TIME, SAME PLACE, LAST ISH! --SUCCINCT STAN
AND NOW, AS SURELY AS THE RAINBOW BRIDGE DOTH STAND, MIRACLES AWAIT THEE--
1

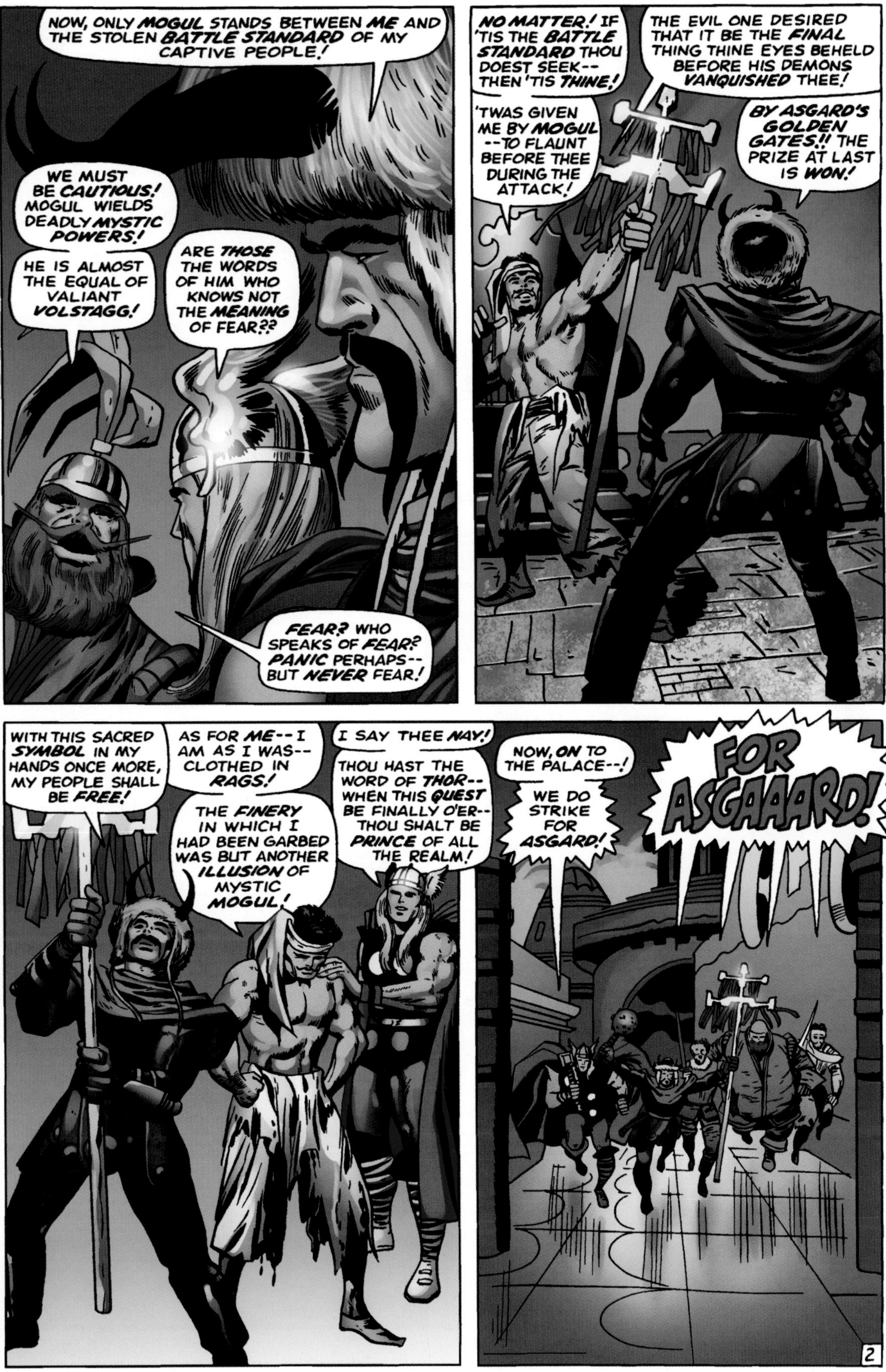
NOW, ONLY MOGUL STANDS BETWEEN ME AND THE STOLEN BATTLE STANDARD OF MY CAPTIVE PEOPLE!
WE MUST BE CAUTIOUS! MOGUL WIELDS DEADLY MYSTIC POWERS!
HE IS ALMOST THE EQUAL OF VALIANT VOLSTAGG!
ARE THOSE THE WORDS OF HIM WHO KNOWS NOT THE MEANING OF FEAR??
FEAR? WHO SPEAKS OF FEAR? PANIC PERHAPS-- BUT NEVER FEAR!
NO MATTER! IF 'TIS THE BATTLE STANDARD THOU DOEST SEEK-- THEN 'TIS THINE!
THE EVIL ONE DESIRED THAT IT BE THE FINAL THING THINE EYES BEHELD BEFORE HIS DEMONS VANQUISHED THEE!
'TWAS GIVEN ME BY MOGUL --TO FLAUNT BEFORE THEE DURING THE ATTACK!
BY ASGARD'S GOLDEN GATES!! THE PRIZE AT LAST IS WON!
WITH THIS SACRED SYMBOL IN MY HANDS ONCE MORE, MY PEOPLE SHALL BE FREE!
AS FOR ME-- I AM AS I WAS-- CLOTHED IN RAGS!
THE FINERY IN WHICH I HAD BEEN GARBED WAS BUT ANOTHER ILLUSION OF MYSTIC MOGUL!
I SAY THEE NAY!
THOU HAST THE WORD OF THOR-- WHEN THIS QUEST BE FINALLY O'ER-- THOU SHALT BE PRINCE OF ALL THE REALM!
NOW, ON TO THE PALACE--!
WE DO STRIKE FOR ASGARD!
FOR ASGAAARD!
2

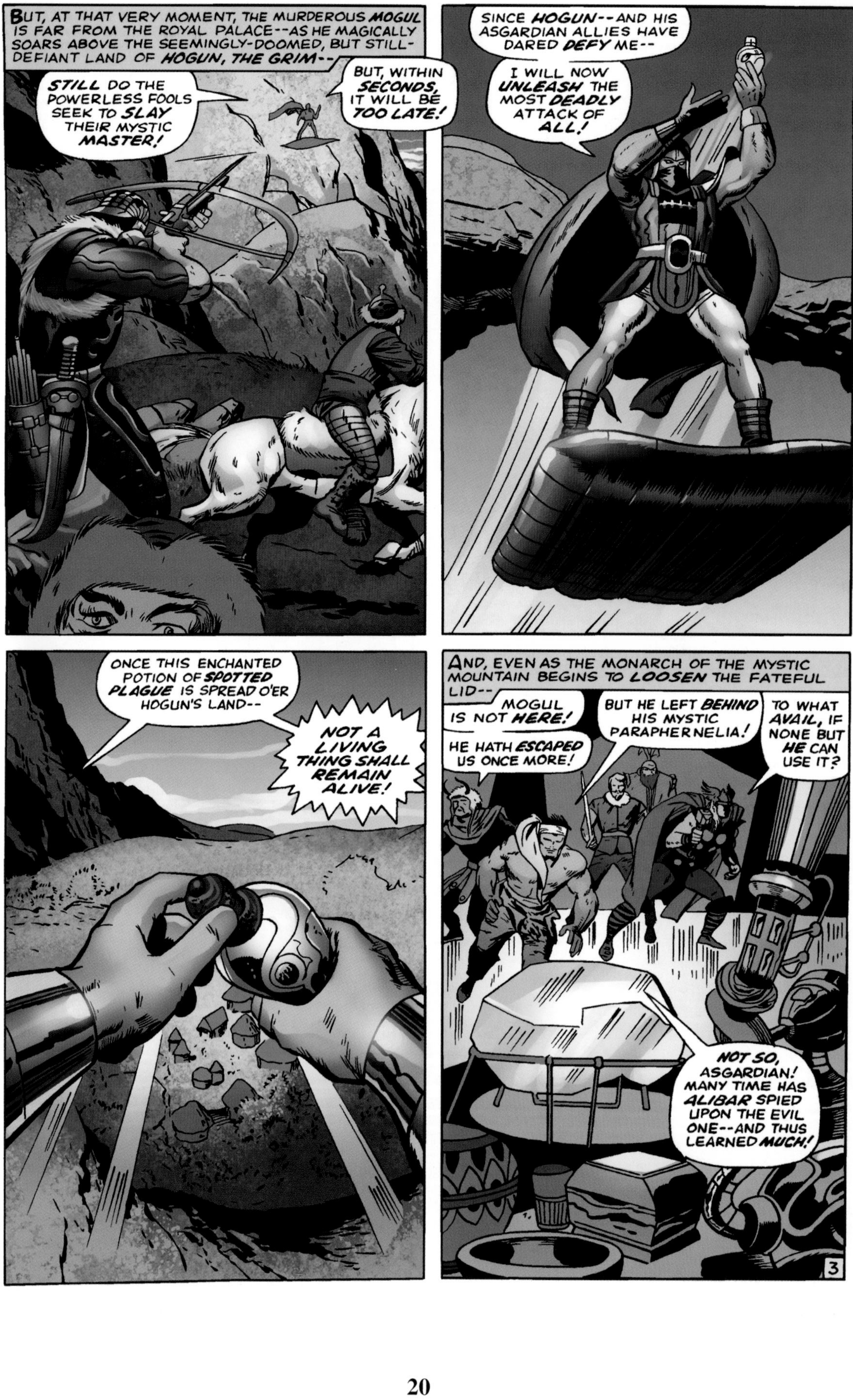

BUT, AT THAT VERY MOMENT, THE MURDEROUS MOGUL IS FAR FROM THE ROYAL PALACE--AS HE MAGICALLY SOARS ABOVE THE SEEMINGLY-DOOMED, BUT STILL-DEFIANT LAND OF HOGUN, THE GRIM--
STILL DO THE POWERLESS FOOLS SEEK TO SLAY THEIR MYSTIC MASTER!
BUT, WITHIN SECONDS, IT WILL BE TOO LATE!
SINCE HOGUN--AND HIS ASGARDIAN ALLIES HAVE DARED DEFY ME--
I WILL NOW UNLEASH THE MOST DEADLY ATTACK OF ALL!
ONCE THIS ENCHANTED POTION OF SPOTTED PLAGUE IS SPREAD O'ER HOGUN'S LAND--
NOT A LIVING THING SHALL REMAIN ALIVE!
AND, EVEN AS THE MONARCH OF THE MYSTIC MOUNTAIN BEGINS TO LOOSEN THE FATEFUL LID--
MOGUL IS NOT HERE!
HE HATH ESCAPED US ONCE MORE!
BUT HE LEFT BEHIND HIS MYSTIC PARAPHERNELIA!
TO WHAT AVAIL, IF NONE BUT HE CAN USE IT?
NOT SO, ASGARDIAN! MANY TIME HAS ALIBAR SPIED UPON THE EVIL ONE--AND THUS LEARNED MUCH!
3

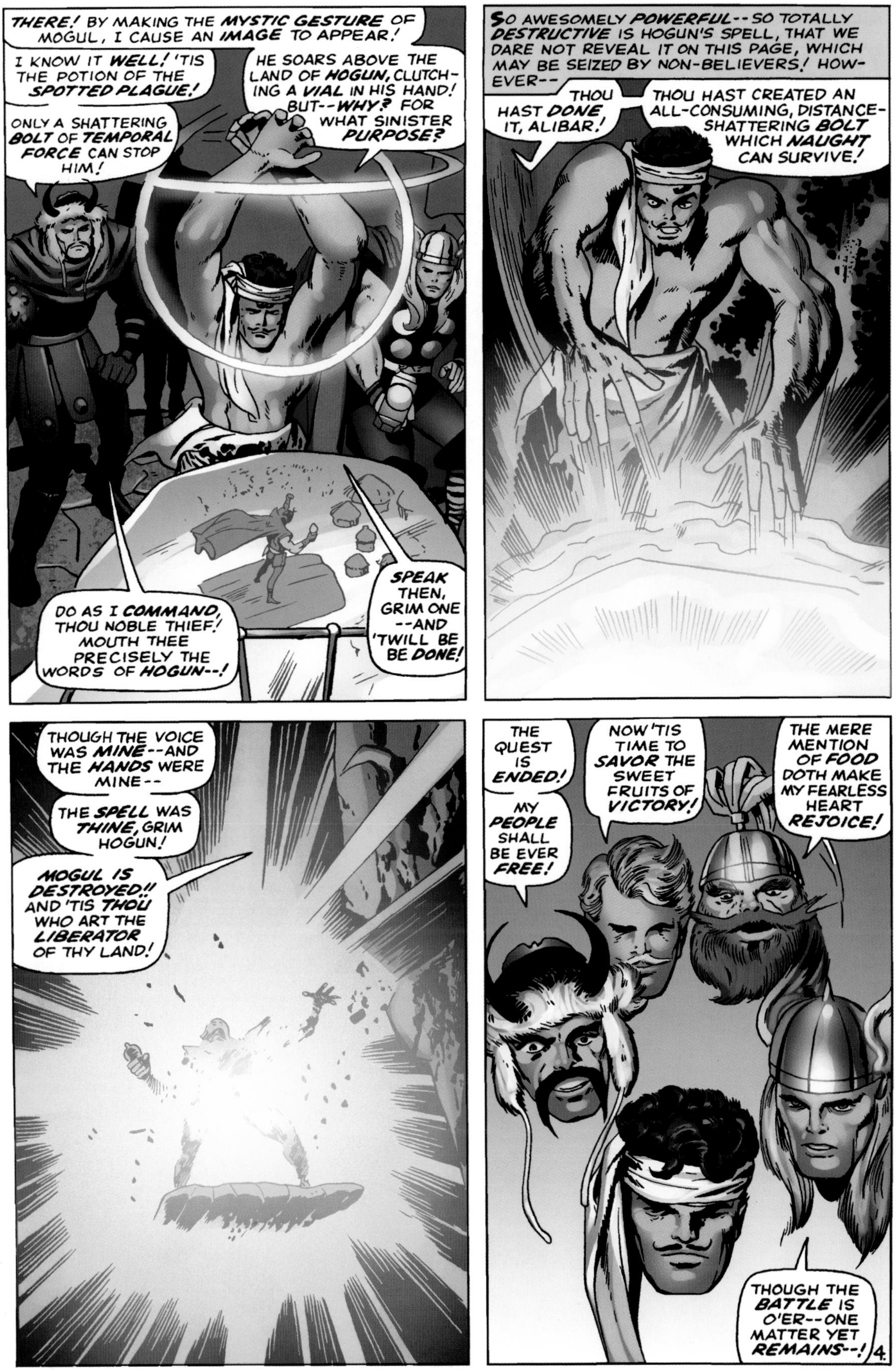
THERE! BY MAKING THE MYSTIC GESTURE OF MOGUL, I CAUSE AN IMAGE TO APPEAR!
I KNOW IT WELL! 'TIS THE POTION OF THE SPOTTED PLAGUE!
HE SOARS ABOVE THE LAND OF HOGUN, CLUTCHING A VIAL IN HIS HAND! BUT--WHY? FOR WHAT SINISTER PURPOSE?
ONLY A SHATTERING BOLT OF TEMPORAL FORCE CAN STOP HIM!
DO AS I COMMAND, THOU NOBLE THIEF! MOUTH THEE PRECISELY THE WORDS OF HOGUN--!
SPEAK THEN, GRIM ONE --AND 'TWILL BE BE DONE!
SO AWESOMELY POWERFUL--SO TOTALLY DESTRUCTIVE IS HOGUN'S SPELL, THAT WE DARE NOT REVEAL IT ON THIS PAGE, WHICH MAY BE SEIZED BY NON-BELIEVERS! HOWEVER--
THOU HAST DONE IT, ALIBAR!
THOU HAST CREATED AN ALL-CONSUMING, DISTANCE-SHATTERING BOLT WHICH NAUGHT CAN SURVIVE!
THOUGH THE VOICE WAS MINE--AND THE HANDS WERE MINE--
THE SPELL WAS THINE, GRIM HOGUN!
MOGUL IS DESTROYED!! AND 'TIS THOU WHO ART THE LIBERATOR OF THY LAND!
THE QUEST IS ENDED!
MY PEOPLE SHALL BE EVER FREE!
NOW 'TIS TIME TO SAVOR THE SWEET FRUITS OF VICTORY!
THE MERE MENTION OF FOOD DOTH MAKE MY FEARLESS HEART REJOICE!
THOUGH THE BATTLE IS O'ER--ONE MATTER YET REMAINS--!
4.

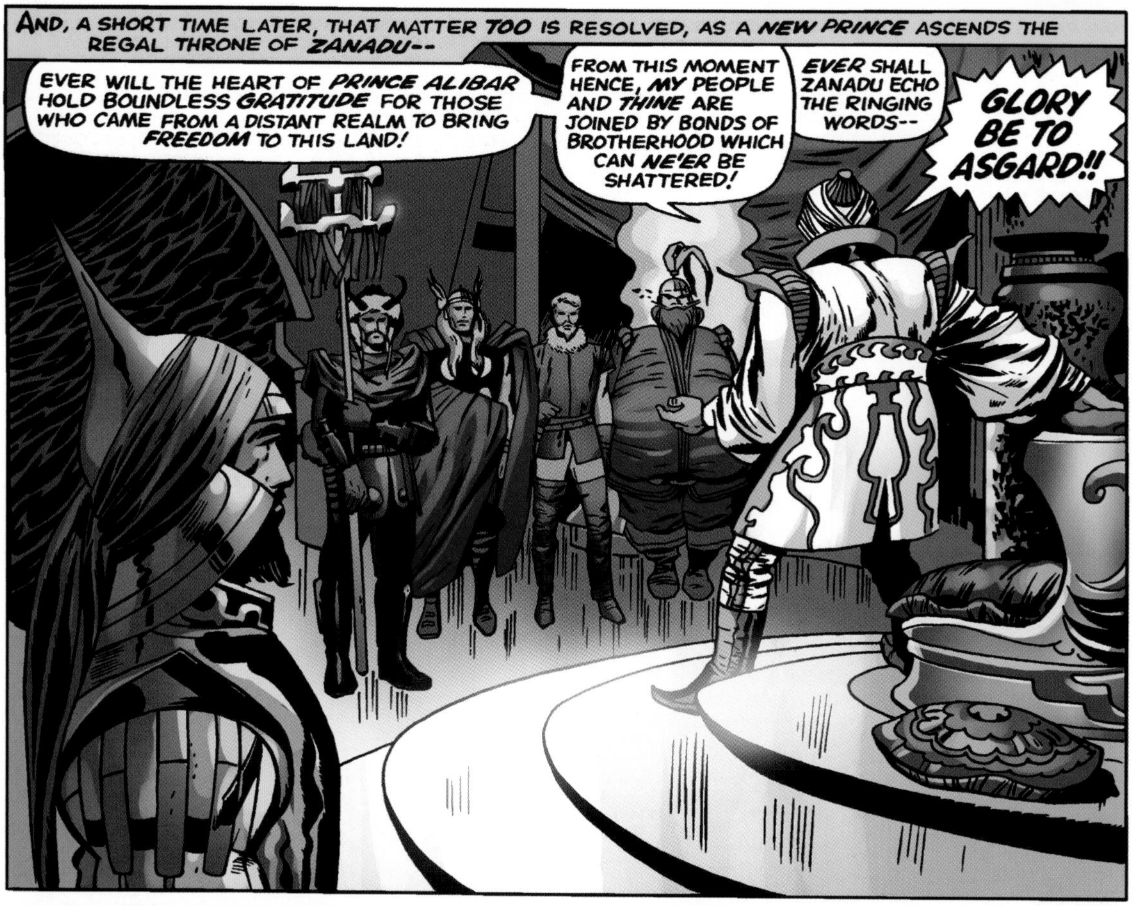
AND, A SHORT TIME LATER, THAT MATTER TOO IS RESOLVED, AS A NEW PRINCE ASCENDS THE REGAL THRONE OF ZANADU--
EVER WILL THE HEART OF PRINCE ALIBAR HOLD BOUNDLESS GRATITUDE FOR THOSE WHO CAME FROM A DISTANT REALM TO BRING FREEDOM TO THIS LAND!
FROM THIS MOMENT HENCE, MY PEOPLE AND THINE ARE JOINED BY BONDS OF BROTHERHOOD WHICH CAN NE'ER BE SHATTERED!
EVER SHALL ZANADU ECHO THE RINGING WORDS--
GLORY BE TO ASGARD!!

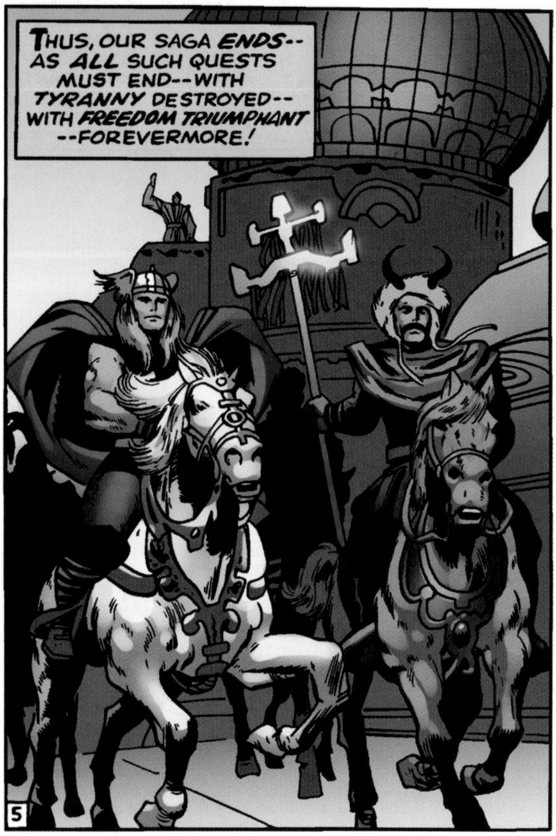
THUS, OUR SAGA ENDS--AS ALL SUCH QUESTS MUST END--WITH TYRANNY DESTROYED--WITH FREEDOM TRIUMPHANT--FOREVERMORE!
5

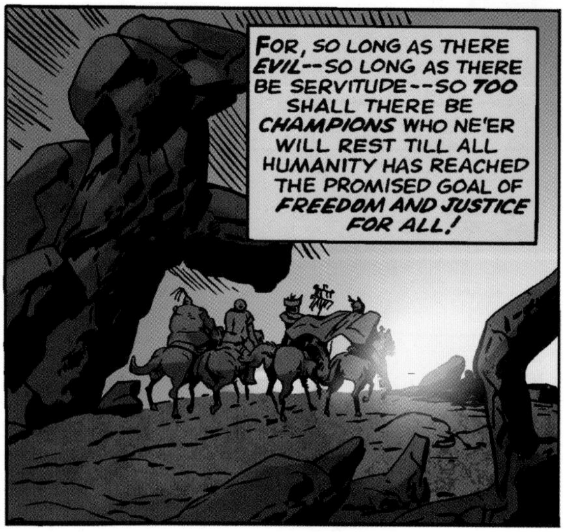
FOR, SO LONG AS THERE EVIL--SO LONG AS THERE BE SERVITUDE--SO TOO SHALL THERE BE CHAMPIONS WHO NE'ER WILL REST TILL ALL HUMANITY HAS REACHED THE PROMISED GOAL OF FREEDOM AND JUSTICE FOR ALL!

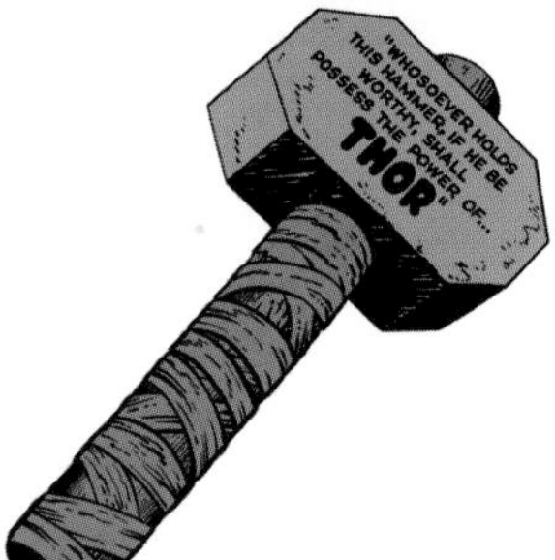
"WHOSOEVER HOLDS THIS HAMMER, IF HE BE WORTHY, SHALL POSSESS THE POWER OF... THOR"

*TALES OF ASGARD #1 (1984)* COVER BY WALTER SIMONSON & MATT MILLA

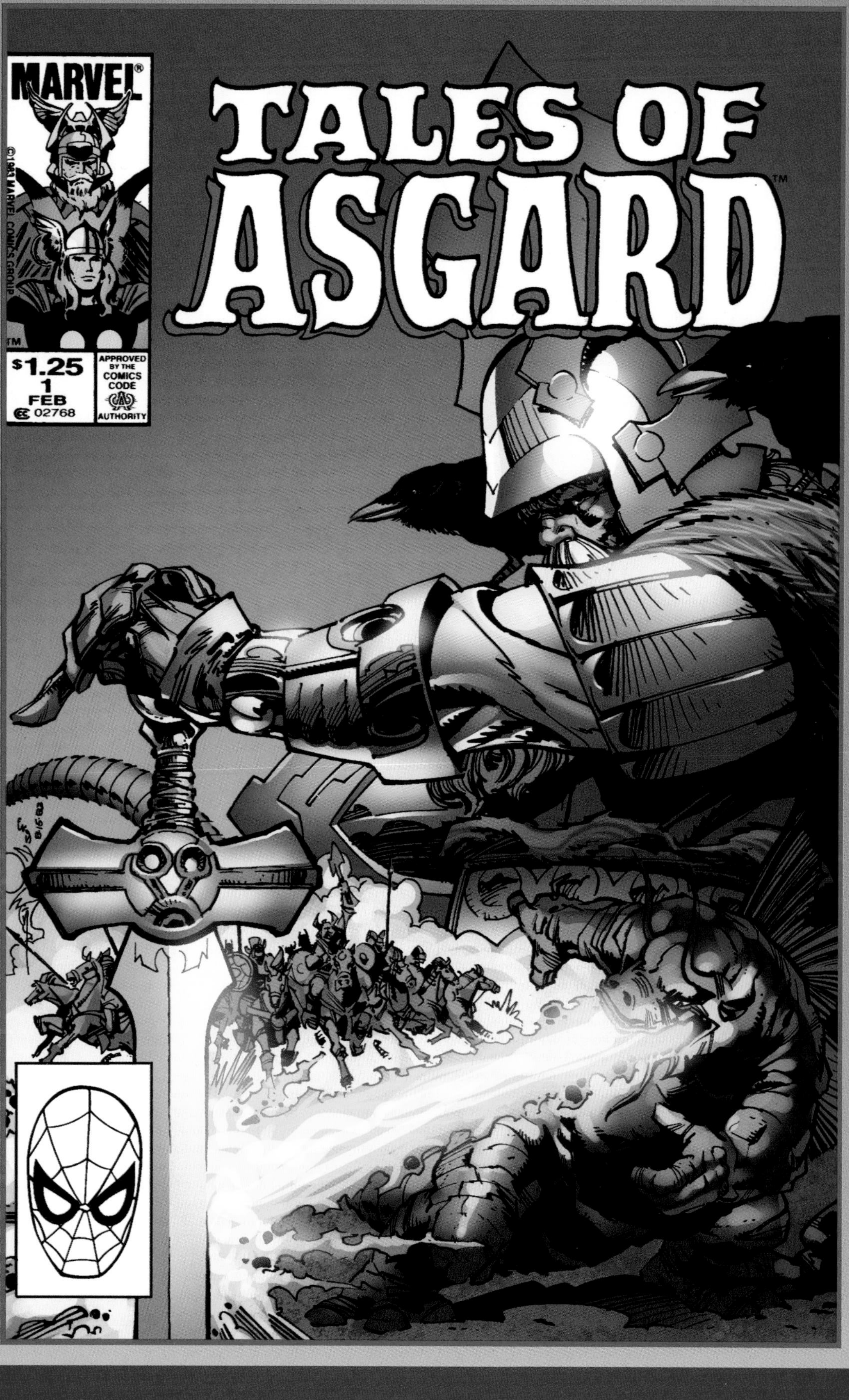
MARVEL®
TALES OF ASGARD™
©1983 MARVEL COMICS GROUP
TM
$1.25
1
FEB
02768
APPROVED BY THE COMICS CODE AUTHORITY

***THOR: TALES OF ASGARD #6*** **ALTERNATE COVER COLORS BY LAURA MARTIN**

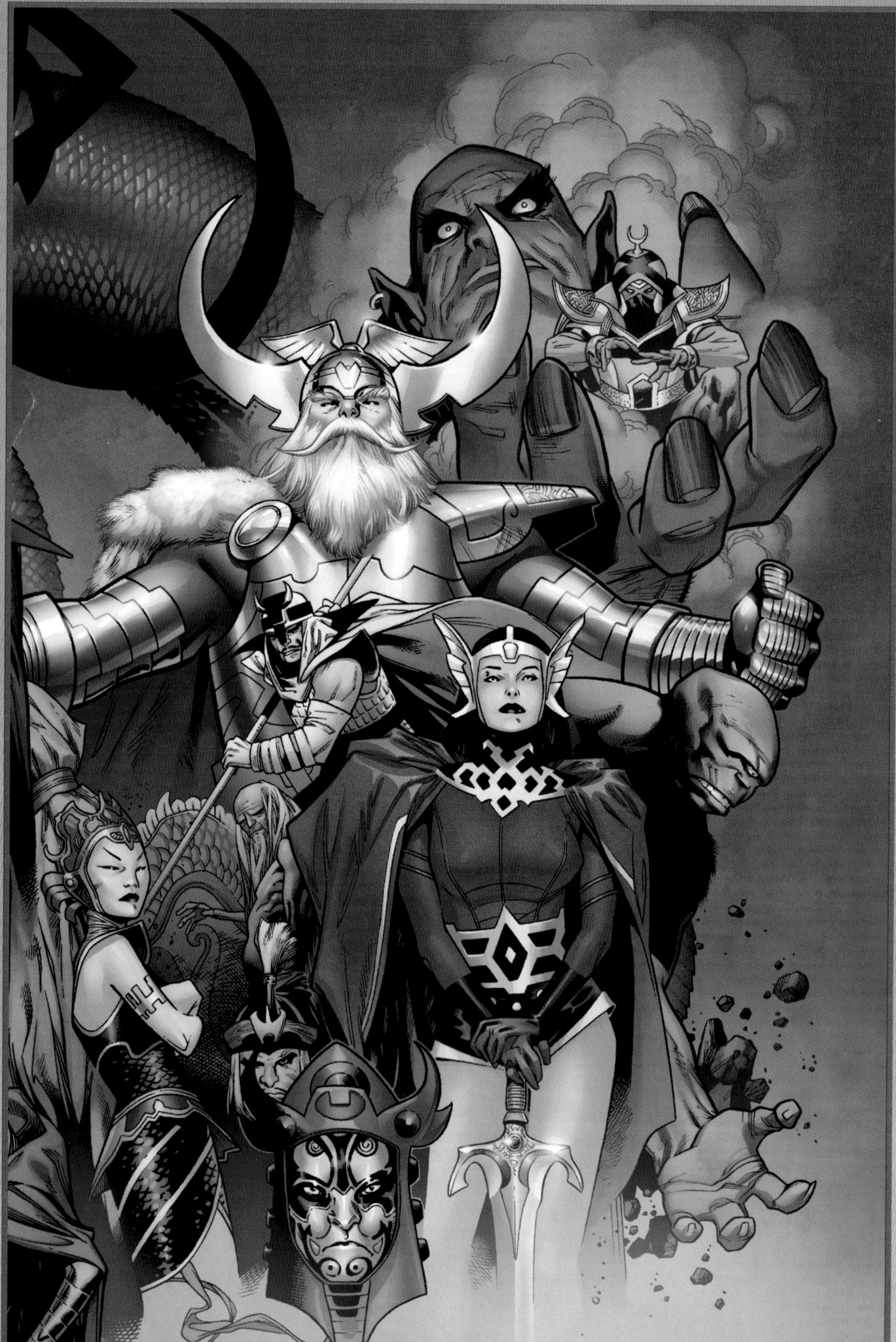